Praise for

"A magnificent feat of imagination, and brilliantly sustained."

– Declan Burke, crime novelist and reviewer

"*Pool of Darkness* rattles along, full of wit and great one-liners, funny along the way, brilliantly researched and imaginatively brought forth. I felt I was getting to know both of these authors / philosophers again. Chandler comes to life as I think he was, generous, but troubled. He comes across as very human, very vulnerable, yet confident in the no-nonsense of his craft – and his relationship with Cissy is sensitive and real."

– Alan Titley, Emeritus Professor of Modern Irish, University College Cork

Also by Tom Sigafoos

The Cursing Stone

CODE BLUE: A Frank Chandler Mystery

(Writing as Tom Brannon)

A Green Christmas Carol

in *Sunshine Superhighway: Solar Sailings*

JayHenge Press

An early version of *Pool of Darkness* was shortlisted for the Penny Dreadful Novella Prize.

Pool of Darkness – Raymond Chandler in Ireland is also available as a Kindle e-book and as an audiobook.

POOL OF DARKNESS

Raymond Chandler in Ireland

A Novel

by

Tom Sigafoos

Pool of Darkness – Raymond Chandler in Ireland
Copyright © 2024 by Dale Thomas Sigafoos

The moral right of Dale Thomas (Tom) Sigafoos to be identified as the Author of the Work has been asserted by him in accordance with the Copyright, Designs, and Patents Act, 1988.

All rights reserved. Apart from any use permitted under Irish, UK, US, and International copyright laws, no part of this publication may be reproduced, stored in a retrieval system, or transmitted, in any form or by any means, without the prior written permission of the author, nor otherwise be circulated in any form of binding or cover other than that in which it is published.

Excerpts from *Pool of Darkness – Raymond Chandler in Ireland* may be quoted in reviews.

This is a work of fiction. Unless otherwise indicated, all the names, characters, businesses, places, events and incidents in this book are either the product of the author's imagination or used in a fictitious manner. Any resemblance to actual persons, living or dead, or actual events is purely coincidental.

ISBN 978-1-4457-3579-5

Revised 1 Oct 2024

Cover image: wacomka / Dreamstime.com. Used with permission.

Writer / Detective Image by Cailin O'Connor, Visual Artist and Illustrator
www.instagram.com/thehealingvisionary
www.instagram.com/cailin_oconnor

Author portrait by John Ford, Cincinnati OH

To Monica

Image by Cailin O'Connor, Visual Artist and Illustrator
www.instagram.com/thehealingvisionary
www.instagram.com/cailin_oconnor

The mystery writer's material is melodrama, which is an exaggeration of violence and fear beyond what one normally experiences in life. (I said normally; no writer ever approximated the life of the Nazi concentration camps.) The means he uses are realistic in the sense that such things happen to people like these and in places like these. But this realism is superficial; the potential of emotion is overcharged, the compression of time and event is a violation of probability, and although such things happen, they do not happen so fast and in such a tight frame of logic to so closely knit a group of people.

– Raymond Chandler,
in a letter to Bernice Baumgarten,
Editor at Brandt and Brandt literary agency

How people can read Mind *(a leading English philosophy journal) if they could read* Street & Smith's Detective Story Magazine *beats me. If philosophy has anything to do with wisdom there's certainly not a grain of that in* Mind, *and quite often a grain in the detective stories.*

– Ludwig Wittgenstein

Chapter One

July 4, 1948

Dear Cissy –
 I miss you.
 I wonder if you're going to tear this up and throw it in the wastebasket. I hope you don't. If I ever get my hands on Mildred I'll wring her neck...

I stopped writing, scratched out the last sentence, and took a sip of my pint. It had been years since I'd handwritten anything, and the dictaphones and secretaries had made me lazy. I lit a cigarette and decided to start in the middle. When people asked me for writing tips, that's what I told them to do.

I'm trying to develop a taste for stout. It tastes like lukewarm milk with a shot of molasses. They give it to pregnant women and recovering drunks...

I scratched out that sentence, too. It didn't seem like a good idea to rub two of my wife's sore spots at the same time.

This is the first quiet moment I've had in Ireland. It took two trains to get from Waterford to Galway, and then a two-hour bus ride to get to Killary Harbor. Renvyle House is full of Americans, and they're the noisiest sons of bitches anyplace they go, so I've headed out into the country to try to find some peace and quiet. Mrs G wasn't thrilled with the idea of letting me drive her car, but the letter from Oliver seems to have done the trick. Driving on the left isn't hard to get used to.

The hotel is a fancy old place full of overstuffed chairs. I wouldn't be surprised if Kipling slept there. Or maybe Oscar Wilde. I hope they washed the sheets if he did.

My pen snagged on a crack in the wooden tabletop and left a blot of ink on the paper. I'd need to copy it over on a smooth surface. I didn't want her to think I was drunk.

I'm in a real country pub, the kind they call a "shebeen." There must be three hundred years of beer and spit and bitter tears soaked into this table, and the seats have been polished by a thousand arses. I wonder what M would make of this place. Nothing in Los Angeles is more than fifty years old, but nothing here is less than a hundred. I ought to bring him over here.

I wondered what she was doing. With an eight-hour time difference, it would be six-thirty in the morning in California. She wouldn't be out of bed yet.

I stuffed the papers into my shirt pocket. I'd stopped leaving first drafts lying around, even letters to my wife. I could imagine myself at a table – not a friendly old table in an Irish pub, but a hard-edged oak table in a high-ceilinged room in front of a bank of politicians with microphones. *This is your handwriting, isn't it? In your affidavit, you said that you didn't know these people, but I see here that you wrote to them...*

I could see myself sweating and stammering, afraid to open my mouth. They'd seize on every word and twist it into my guts. And if I didn't say anything, they'd nail me as a hostile witness.

Cissy had tried to reassure me. *Why would they come after you, Ray? You've never had anything to do with Communists. Or have you?*

Christ Almighty, no! But don't you know what the studio would do if I had to testify? Aren't you on my side here?

Of course I am. But I just think that you're worrying unnecessarily...

I thought about telling her about Sam Berkowitz, but I didn't. Her lungs were giving her trouble, and I didn't want to add to her miseries.

I'd read Sam's letter so many times that it fell apart at the creases.

June 17, 1948

Ray,

Thanks a million for writing to me. You can't imagine what it's like being stuck in here and waiting for the mail. I feel like a starving rat. If I get a letter, my day lights up like a Christmas tree. If I don't, a door slams shut in my head and I don't want to talk to anybody.

Honest to God, I'd give my left arm to be able to meet you at Musso and Frank's, just to sit and kvetch about our publishers like we used to. And grouse about our agents and the studios and our wives. Instead I get to listen to a bunch of convicts talk baseball. Otherwise, I get to mop the fucking floor.

At least Rose and the kids are all right. They're getting a dribble of royalties, and Wilder, bless his bony ass, has been sending them checks. He's claiming that they're advances on some future screenplay. Hey, we had some fun working on *Double Indemnity*, didn't we? I know you didn't get along with him very well. Maybe it was easier for me as a landsman.

Yes, I wish I hadn't shot off my mouth during the hearing. But that bastard Parnell Thomas got under my skin. It was the way he kept stringing out my name. Tell me, Mis-ter Berk-o-witz... He might as well have branded a Star of David on my forehead. I thought we just fought a war to put a stop to that Nazi shit, and I told him so. I used those words. My lawyer tried to stop me, but I didn't care. They were goddamned right I was in Contempt of Congress. I still am. And if anybody is reading my mail, you can quote me.

So now I sit here in Leavenworth with a cross-section of American scumbags. They tell me that it would be a lot worse in a State Pen, everything from the food to the guards. For this I'm supposed to be grateful?

This place would be tolerable, Ray, if it weren't for the psychos. Nasty sons of bitches, crazy as hell, they ought to be in some kind of joint for the criminally insane, but they've ended up in here. There's one musclebound redneck who calls himself Snake and goes around muttering "I'm gonna fuck me a nigger and a kike." I pity any guy who gets cornered by him.

As soon as I put this in the mail, I'll think of a dozen things that I'll wish I'd remembered to tell you. Whatever happens, Ray, don't give them a reason to stick you in a place like this. Eat a mile of shit if you need to. Tell them you think America is the greatest country in the world. Tell them that you were seduced by Emma Goldman, or somebody else who's dead.

Whatever you do, don't let them get under your skin.

Your friend,
Sam

Sam Berkowitz, rewrite guy, my pal. He must have thought he'd improve his chances by calling himself *Berkshire*. A cocky little guy who could do great impressions of Jimmy Cagney and Groucho Marx. His ideas for screenplays were corny as vaudeville, but he had bottomless reserves of nervous energy, and he'd work for long hours after I fogged over and went home. I liked him. He was one of the few people I knew who wasn't always trying to pick my pocket.

I wrote back to try to cheer him up with some publishing gossip and a few limp jokes. Two weeks later an official envelope arrived in the mail, returning my letter along with a letter from the Justice Department. *We regret to inform you that Prisoner Samuel Berkowitz has died in custody.*

I had to drink a bottle of scotch before I could put my imagination to sleep that night. I hated the idea that Sam had been locked up with a musclebound redneck, and I hated the idea that the Feds had written a letter that linked me with him. My agent told me that a lot of people were burning their old documents and letters. Mine were sitting in a filing cabinet in California, along with the other loose ends of my life.

The man who opened the pub door didn't look like an Irishman. He stood blinking at the threshold, a skinny guy with curly hair. He wasn't carrying a gun, or anything else. He wore rumpled black pants and a white shirt that looked like he'd slept in it. But they were city clothes, not the threadbare hand-me-downs that most people wore around Killary Harbor.

The door swung shut behind him, and he blinked as his eyes adjusted to the dim light. The two old lads took long sips of their pints and studied his reflection in the cracked mirror behind the whiskey bottles. He took a seat on a bar-stool, wincing as it scraped across the stone floor.

The bartender glanced up from his newspaper and said, "Are yez all right?"

The curly-haired man said, "I would like to have a pilsener." He pronounced *have* like a German. *Haff.*

The bartender said, "I can't serve you now."

"Why?"

"It's the Holy Hour."

The curly-haired man stiffened. "What exactly does that mean?" *Vot.*

The bartender stood up. "I can't pull any pints from two to three in the afternoon. If the *Gardaí* catch me at it, I'll lose my license."

The curly-haired man glanced around the room. He looked a little like John Garfield. He pointed at the two men at the bar and said, "But they are drinking."

"I pulled them pints before two."

"And if I come back after three…"

"I can serve you then. But not before."

The curly-haired man started toward the door, but he turned back. "Do you have pilsener?"

The bartender exchanged glances with the old lads, and silence hung in the room.

I said, "They have lager." Everybody turned to look at me. I said, "It's not as yeasty as pilsener, but it's pretty good."

The curly-haired man nodded at me and said, "Thank you," as he walked out the door. *Tank.*

It was quiet for a while. The bartender turned to me and pitched his voice a little louder. "You know him, do you?"

"I never saw him before in my life."

One of the old boys rolled a cigarette and lit it with a wooden match. The bartender said, "Who's yer man, Paddy?"

The older fellow took a long swallow of Guinness. "He's livin' out there in the Doctor's cottage at Rosroe. By the harbour."

"Been keeping an eye on him, have you?"

"I been by there every day, but I haven't seen him. Or nobody."

The younger one said, "Did you look?"

"Well, I didn't *look*, but I didn't *not* look, either." No one said anything. "I mean, if you go by somewhere, and there's a soul living there, it *looks* like they're living there. They hang out the washing. Do you know what I mean? There's smoke coming out of the chimney."

"Ah, sure, Paddy. Unless he seen you coming and put out the lights."

"Well, you're a fine one to talk. You're the one that's been barred from every pub in Tullycross…"

A horse-drawn wagon clopped by on the road outside. "I'll tell you one thing," said Paddy. "That bloke hasn't been hanging out any washing. He's been wearing them same clothes for a month."

"I guess he goes to the same wash-house you do, then…"

"Feck it, you know what I mean! He's not like us! Anyway, I know where he's from."

"How would you know that?"

"When I come back from Letterfrack yesterday, Liam give me his post. Asked me to drop it in to him."

"And you did?"

"And I did."

"So what did he say to you?"

"He wasn't at home. I put it through the door."

A fly buzzed against the windowpane. The bartender said, "So who is he, then?"

"I didn't read his post. "

"But what did it say on the envelope?"

Paddy smiled like a man who's hooked a fish. "It's from that school where the Doctor gets letters from. You know – where Liam was stationed during the Emergency."

"In England? So he's a Brit?"

"No, he's got a German name."

"What is it?"

"I couldn't read it clear. It's Wittenberg, or Weisenstein, or something like that."

"If it's Weisenstein," the bartender said, "he ain't German." He looked across the room at me. "Wouldn't you say so?"

I didn't say anything. I was thinking about what Hubert Butler had told me.

The *Vancouver* had moored at the Waterford docks in the early morning. The chess game still sat on the galley table, and I studied the board while I ate eggs and sausages from a chipped enamel plate. Billings and I had worked ourselves into a tight convergence of knights, rooks, and a bishop in the corner — my king's corner. Then Billings had been called to the bridge when a storm blew up, and the unfinished game sat where we'd left it. I was in a tight spot, but I thought that with enough time and concentration I might find a counteroffensive to take the pressure off.

I was alone in the galley. I could hear the ship groan as the dock-winches lifted the cargo pallets from the hold. Mostly lumber, Billings had said – Canadian lumber. Irish forests had been stripped bare by two centuries of English shipbuilding. I wondered how much it would cost to buy a two-by-four in Ireland after it had been carried a third of the way around the world.

Billings opened the galley door and grinned. "I was hoping you hadn't left yet." He helped himself to a cup of black coffee from a tall urn. "Want some?"

"Sure. Thanks."

He sat down across the table from me. I wondered if he'd seen me on the foredeck last night. He said, "I'm going to be up to my arse for the rest of the day. As soon as we get this lumber off, we're taking on a load of slates."

"Slates?"

"Roof slates. Bangor Blues. They can't get enough of them on the West Coast."

"Sounds like you're in the right business."

"The shipping is easy. The paperwork's a nightmare. Anyway, I wanted to say that it's been good sailing with you."

I squirmed a little. I started to say, *Well, I appreciate...* but I got stuck. I didn't want to sound like a pompous ass. *You've been very generous...? I appreciate what you and the crew...?* Finally I said, "I wondered if you'd think that passengers on a freighter were a pain in the neck."

"Some of them are. You aren't."

"Well, thanks. I appreciate..." I got stuck again.

He stood up and drained his coffee cup. My stutters didn't seem to bother him. He grinned and said, "Whose butt am I supposed to kick on the chessboard now?"

"My God."

He looked puzzled. "Did I say something wrong?"

"No, not at all. But you're the second person who's said that to me."

"Somebody on the crew?"

"No. Somebody I knew a long time ago."

We shook hands and he left, but my blurt and his question still hung in the air. Two crewmen came into the galley, pulled coffees for themselves and sat at another table. We ignored each other. Apart from Billings, I hadn't gotten to know anyone on the ship. I drank my coffee and stared at the chessboard, wondering if I'd ever be able to fall into easy companionship with other people.

They always looked uncomfortable, a little edgy when I tried. I was sixty years old, and I still hadn't figured it out.

I stepped off the gangplank. A crewman pointed me toward a customs-and-immigration building at the end of a long, busy wharf. I lugged my suitcases along the dock, avoiding the fork-lift trucks and the stevedores with the dolly-carts. Ships were lined up like railroad cars, disgorging building supplies, food, automobiles and construction equipment. I'd heard the cynics who claimed that it was the war, not the New Deal, that ended the Depression. If they were right, it had been a hell of a price to pay. But it was over, and Ireland seemed to be enjoying an economic bounce. I wondered if they'd buy more of my books.

Dust from the cargo pallets swirled around the wharf, and some of the stevedores wore masks. The corners of my mouth were gritty. I thought about writing a piece on travel-by-freighter – the functional, un-fussy cabins, the cafeteria-tray dinners with the crew, the taciturn conversations of men who worked together in close quarters. None of the ass-kissing or tip-weaseling that you'd get on a passenger ship. I'd filled a notebook with vignettes and ideas on the voyage over. But I missed my typewriter. I'd left it in California, when I was in too much of a hurry to leave.

I put down my suitcases to catch my breath in a nook between two stacks of lumber. I hadn't taken care of myself for years, and I could feel it. I'd been too busy tending to Cissy. Not that she'd demanded it – she would run herself into the ground before she'd ask for help. But we'd fallen into an arrangement – an unspoken one, like most of our arrangements – and I spent my time taking care of the housework and the drudgery. I wondered how she and her sister were doing. I wondered what I was doing.

I lit a cigarette and envied the workmen. I envied anybody who knew where he stood, who could settle into a job, who could put his feet up at the end of a day and feel like he'd accomplished something. I felt like I was operating through a fog, half-listening but not entirely there, holding myself back and out of reach. Sometimes I wondered if I was growing feeble-minded. I'd find myself drifting off in the middle of a sentence, wondering what I'd started to say. I'd see other people's disappointed eyes, and I'd try to shut up before I made a complete ass of myself.

A hat, an expensive fedora with a black band, rolled across the wharf and landed at my feet. Somebody shouted *I know who you are, you son of a bitch!* and somebody's head hit the concrete with a thud. The stevedores pulled a struggling man off another man who was trying to get up from the ground. The man on the ground, a bald guy in a leather jacket, was bleeding from his nose and from a gash on the side of his head. The struggling man, a young guy wearing a brown topcoat and a necktie, was doing the shouting. *Why aren't you in jail, you Nazi bastard? I'll break your neck, I swear to God...*

The bald guy limped as the stevedores led him away. An older man in a grey topcoat walked over to me, picked up the hat from the concrete and shook the dust from it. He looked at me with world-weary eyes for a few seconds before he turned around and walked back to the young guy. *Mind yourself, Reuben,* I could half-hear him saying. *The important thing is for you to get on that ship...*

I'll kill that son of a bitch if he's on my ship!
Settle down, now. Think about where you're going...
Reuben stopped struggling with the stevedores, shook his head, and took back his hat. The older man in the grey topcoat put an arm around his shoulders and kept talking to him in a fatherly way. He nodded to the stevedores, and they drifted back to their work. The two men walked down the wharf past the line of ships until they were obscured in the flurry of fork-lifts and pallets and dust.

A crowd of passengers from an ocean liner had beaten me to the immigration shed, and the lines to the officials' desks were long. I sat on a bench outside and lit another cigarette. A mist was blowing in from the harbor, and it smelled great. There was a word for that. *Petrichor.* I'd smelled *petrichor* when I was a kid, prowling around the docks and the narrow streets near the Waterford harbor. In those days I'd wanted to sail somewhere – anywhere. But instead of stowing away, I'd retreat to one of the bookstores and pick up something to read. I was a timid loner, even then.

"I hope we haven't given you the wrong impression of Ireland."

The man with the grey topcoat was standing by the bench, dusting himself off. He looked to be about fifty, with a prosperous, confident air. He wore expensive-looking shoes that were covered with dust. My wife had taught me to look at other people's shoes.

He seemed friendly enough. I said, "I wondered if we'd landed in Donnybrook."

"You'd think so, wouldn't you?" He smiled. "My friend doesn't normally get into brawls."

"He looks like he could take care of himself if he did."

"He certainly can. But the authorities might take a dim view."

"What was the fuss about, then?"

The man took off his hat and ran his fingers through his hair. "That is quite a long story."

"I'm going to be sitting here for at least half an hour. I've got nothing but time. Join me?"

"Thank you. I will." He dusted the other half of the bench with a handkerchief and sat down. "My name is Hubert Butler. Do I detect an American accent?"

"You do. But that's a long story, too."

He looked at me closely. "You aren't Jewish, no?"

"No. My parents were Irish, but I was born in America." I looked at him more carefully. He looked a little like Seán O'Casey, the playwright. I said, "Is your friend Jewish?"

"Yes. And that's what the bother was about." He massaged the bridge of his nose. "Where to begin?"

"Well, how do you know him?"

He turned and looked at me. "I met him and his parents in Austria in 1940."

I looked at him more carefully. "What were you doing there?"

He took off his glasses and wiped them with a handkerchief. "I'd worked in eastern European countries all through the Thirties, and I'd seen the Nazis stirring up a wave of anti-Jewish agitation. Then after the *Anschluss*, the gloves came off and they started sending Austrian Jews to labour camps. That was when..." He paused for a second. "That was when many of us began trying to help them escape."

"To escape to Ireland?"

"No, I'm afraid that's one of the painful parts. Ireland wouldn't accept Jewish refugees in those years. Unless..."

"Unless what?"

"Unless they converted to Catholicism. It was not one of my country's proudest moments."

We sat there for a while. I said, "The rest of the world doesn't have a lot of high ground to stand on, either. Remember the *St. Louis*? A whole damned steamship full of Jewish refugees, and nobody would take them in. Not the US, not Cuba, not even Canada. They sent them back to Germany, and most of them died in the gas chambers."

The man said, "I know." We sat there for a while longer. Then he said, "A few of us tried to do what the governments wouldn't do. We used the Old School Tie and every other connection we could imagine to arrange for visas and transportation. That was when I brought Reuben and his family to Ireland."

"But I thought you just said..."

"We brought them in on tourist visas, just to get them out of the Third Reich. Then we pulled strings to arrange for permanent visas in other countries wherever we could. The Quakers were particularly helpful."

"No kidding? My mother was a Quaker. From here."

"My God. What was her name?"

"Florence Thornton. Her brother was a lawyer."

"Then your uncle was Ernest Thornton?"

I started to say *That was him*, but I heard an echo of my mother's voice. *You say too much to people, Raymond. You shouldn't tell them so much.* I glanced at Butler and saw him studying me with an uneasy stare. I cleared my throat and said, "So what was that fistfight about?"

He hesitated for a second before he said, "Reuben was a commando in the Army. His parents went on to America in 1940, but he wanted to stay and fight."

"So that's why he looks like he could take care of himself."

"Yes, he does." He looked down ruefully at his dust-covered shoes. "Have you been following the developments in England since the war?"

"I'm afraid that Americans are too busy patting ourselves on the back to pay attention to the rest of the world. I know they dropped Churchill..."

"I'm talking about the Black Shirts. Do you know about Oswald Mosley?"

I had blurry memories of some kind of Nazi sympathizers marching in England in the Thirties. "I've heard of his name. Are the Black Shirts still around?"

"I'm afraid so. They started holding rallies in East London as soon as the war was over."

"Really? You'd think they'd slink off with their tails between their legs..."

"Their neck has been unimaginable."

"Their *neck*?"

"Their effrontery. Their arrogance."

I said, "That's where the reptiles have their brains, isn't it? Their necks?"

He turned and smiled at me. "Reuben would like that one. He thinks they're evolutionary throwbacks. He says we can beat them, but we can't quite kill them." He pulled a folded pamphlet out of his coat pocket. "If you're interested, here's what Reuben has been up to in London."

I looked at the title of the pamphlet. *The 43 Group Fights Fascism Today.* I said, "Is this from the Anti-Defamation League?"

Butler chuckled. "Hardly. It's an organisation of ex-commandos who break up Fascist rallies."

"How? By heckling?"

"They don't waste time doing that. They push through the crowd and knock over the microphones. Physically."

"But don't the Fascists fight back?"

"Not as much as you might think. And Reuben and his friends don't mind a few split lips." He handed me the pamphlet. "Take this. It's quite a story."

"Thanks – I'll read it. What do the Quakers think about this?"

Butler looked down at the ground again. "There is a time for Quakers," he said, "and there is a time for commandos."

I looked at Hubert Butler in his expensive clothes and dusty shoes. "So what happened back there on the dock?"

"Reuben recognised that man from a dust-up in London. He's a Black Shirt from Stoke Newington."

I looked up at the ships, and the men on the busy wharf. "What's Reuben doing here?"

"He came over to say goodbye to me. He's going to see his parents in New York, and then he'll be on his way to Israel. His skills will be useful there."

A freighter gave a blast from its whistle. The stevedores loosened its lines from the cleats on the dock, and a tugboat edged the prow of the big ship toward open water. I thought about asking Butler what the guy from Stoke Newington was doing in Waterford, but I decided to let it go. I said, "Do you ever wish that people would just sit at home and listen to the radio?"

Butler smiled. "Wasn't it Pascal who expressed that sentiment, or something like it?"

"Did he?"

"It's a fine idea, but I doubt that it would solve our problems. Hitler was very clever in using the radio, you know."

"So was Roosevelt."

"So was Churchill." He half-turned to me. "I don't mean to pry, but I'm fairly certain that I recognise you." I didn't say anything. He said, "I believe that I've seen your photo on the dust-jackets of crime novels."

Another voice in the back of my head said *No – you can't let this happen*. I looked away. "People are always telling me that."

"That's a pity. I enjoy those books very much. I'm a writer myself."

"Crime novels?"

"No, I work in a different vein. Other kinds of crimes."

"What kinds?"

He started to say something, but he seemed to change his mind. He said, "They have a saying in Czechoslovakia. *The big thieves hang the little ones.*" He took a card from his wallet and handed it to me. We stood up and shook hands, but I couldn't quite meet his eye. He said, "Are you staying in Waterford?"

I hesitated again. He seemed like a profoundly decent man. I wanted to tell him who I was, why I was alone, how much I yearned for a friend. But my mother's wisp of caution still plucked at my sleeve. Butler had been brave, but he had the backup and connections of an aristocrat – *the Old School Tie* – and the confidence that no one would try to whisk him away in the dark of night. None of the worries that kept the rest of us from sticking our necks out.

I said, "No, I'm headed for Galway."

He looked me over for a moment. He said, "Well, I hope that you enjoy your time in Ireland," and he walked off. I fought back an impulse to follow him. I hadn't even told him my name.

On the train to Galway, I read the 43 Group pamphlet and its potted biography of Oswald Mosley. Born into a rich family, he had organized the Black Shirts in England in the Thirties, hoping to take over Britain and strike an alliance with the Nazis. He married his second wife, another English blue-blood, in Germany in 1936, and Hitler was their guest of honor. The government locked him up when hostilities broke out, but he wangled a release in 1943.

After the war, Mosley started holding Black Shirt rallies again. There had been a recession, with layoffs, and he blamed it on the Jews. The British police had protected the Black Shirts at first, out of a dogged British tradition of protecting free speech. But the Jewish ex-servicemen of London decided that enough was enough, and they pushed through the crowds and knocked over the microphones and stopped the bastards from broadcasting their ugly ideas.

I put the pamphlet down and looked out the train window at the green Irish fields and the stone walls and the lakes. I'd been a soldier, too. How many fascist rallies had I broken up?

From the door of the shebeen I could see the curly-haired man walking along the road toward the harbor. *Harbour*, I reminded myself. Over here you *labour* at the *harbour* with your *neighbou*. Waste of ink.

I walked to the car and opened the passenger door before I remembered that I was on the wrong side. I walked around the front and wiped at a smudge on the hood. Gogarty had terrible taste in cars in America, and I could see that he'd developed it in Ireland. He'd bought his wife a yellow monster of a Rolls-Royce with chrome running boards and a rosewood dashboard and a fancy hood ornament that looked like a statue. Somebody called it a "saloon." I kept looking for the bartender.

I caught up with him at the curve where the road skirted a sheer cliff that dropped into the sea. He was standing at the edge of the cliff, looking down at a cluster of black birds that were perched on the rocks. I rolled down the window and said, "Want a lift?"

Without looking up, he said, "Do you know the name of those birds?"

I leaned out the car window to try to see them better. "I'm not sure. They might be cormorants. Or maybe gannets."

He looked down at them and said, "They look like priests."

"Maybe they're penguins waiting for their tuxedoes to come back from the cleaners."

He looked at me suspiciously, and I wondered if I'd pushed something too far. But then he said, "You are making a joke, yes?"

"I'm making an attempt at a joke."

"An attempt? I have been thinking about jokes."

"If you have to think about them too much, they aren't funny."

He smiled. "I have been thinking about thinking, too."

I said, "*In your thinking make not thought your aim.*"

He frowned. "Do you really mean that?"

"Not really. I'm just quoting."

"Quoting?"

"Kipling. Would you like a lift?"

"What do you mean?"

"A ride in the car. To wherever you're going."

"Yes, please. I would appreciate that."

He opened the door, and I picked up my copy of *The High Window* from the passenger seat and tossed it into the back. He saw the book and looked at me briefly before he sat down and stared out the front window. He had the same severe ecclesiastical air as the birds. I said, "Where to?"

"I am living by the harbour."

"You were looking for a pilsener a few minutes ago. I think we might find one at the hotel."

"Is it not the Holy Hour there, too?"

"I don't know. I've been here a few days, and nobody's said anything about it before. What's your name?"

"Ludwig Wittgenstein," he said. "And what is yours?"

"Ray Thornton. Good to meet you."

We shook hands. He had a dry, cautious grip like a pianist. I turned the car around and headed down the road toward the hotel. He said, "You are not Irish, are you?"

"I'm from the US. But my mother was Irish. What about you?"

He paused again before he spoke. "I am from *Wien.*"

"Where?"

"*Vien-na.* Although I have spent many years in England." We rolled along the road for a few minutes before he said, "How do you think Irish people feel about Jews?"

I didn't know what to say. I said, "Have you read *Ulysses?*"

"Some of it. I prefer Tolstoy."

"Do you remember the scene with the schoolmaster? *Mister Dedalus, Ireland has the honour of being the only country that has never persecuted the Jews. And do you know why? Because she never let them in.*"

He stared out the window for a long time. "Is that supposed to be a joke?"

"I think so. I really don't know."

"My mother was Catholic," he said, "and my father was a Jew."

"Did you think that the Holy Hour business was just an excuse..."

We sat in an awkward silence. He said, "I am only wondering how Irish people feel..."

I said, "I don't know how anybody feels about anybody. Where I come from, everybody's trying to pick everybody else's pocket. They'll use anything to try to get the jump on you. If you're Jewish, they'll use that. If you're Catholic, they'll use that. They're all trying to be shrewd and tough, but most of them are broke and lonely. I don't know what anybody thinks over here."

He thought for a minute before he said, "Did you know that the President of Ireland sent condolences to Germany when Hitler died?"

"You've got to be kidding."

"Not at all. They were neutral during the War."

"I'll bet that went over like a fart in church. The condolences, I mean."

He looked at me with a gleam in his eye. "You're Raymond Chandler, aren't you?"

I said, "Who's he?"

Chapter Two

We pulled into the parking lot in front of the Renvyle House Hotel. A bald man in a leather jacket was trimming the rhododendrons at the side of the hotel. I looked to see if he had a bandage on his head, or bloodstains on his clothes. He didn't.

I made a project out of cruising the gravelled area and easing the Rolls in slowly between an Austin and a tree. Wittgenstein waited until I finished fiddling with the car before he spoke. "You are the author of that book."

"What book?"

"The one on the rear seat."

"I wish I was. No, my friend, I'm in the oil business."

He looked down at his hands in his lap. "Then why are you here? There is no oil in Ireland."

"You're right about that. There might be some down in the shale, but it'll be a hundred years before we need to squeeze it up." I started to reach for a cigarette in the glove compartment, but I thought better of it. I said, "I'm here because my wife threw me out."

He glanced at me. "Why did she do that?"

"Because I was chasing skirt." He looked down again, and I wondered if I'd skidded too far into the vernacular. I said, "I got involved with a girl at the office. Bad policy. You should never get your meat and potatoes from the same store." He still looked down. I said, "Do you know what I'm talking about?"

"I know what you mean. But I do not know if I entirely believe you."

"You could ask my wife, if you want to. But she's in California."

He thought for a minute and then nodded. "All right, Mister Ray Thornton, you are in the oil business. But I am disappointed. I wish you were the author of that book. I like American detective stories."

"No kidding? I like them too. Which ones?"

"My favourite is *Rendezvous with Fear* by Norbert Davis."

I began to feel a hot flush on the back of my neck, the way it feels when you're lying. I lit a cigarette and opened the door. Wittgenstein said, "Do you know it?"

"The book? Yeah, I read it a few years ago. It's about the guy with the dog, isn't it?"

"Yes. His name is Doan, and his only friend is a Great Dane named Carstairs." He turned his head and glanced at the book in the back seat. "Philip Marlowe has no friends, does he?"

"No, he doesn't. Let's go get those beers we were talking about."

Nobody seemed to have told the Renvyle House bartender about the Holy Hour legislation. The bar looked like an English men's club, or at least what I'd always imagined an English men's club would look like. There were fancy plaster-cast moldings around the edges of the ceilings – probably spelled *mouldings* by the locals – and there were more *mouldings* around the chandeliers, and around the wall sconces, and every other damned place they could find to stick them. Maps lined the walls – maps of County Galway, of Ireland, of the British Isles. A brass ashtray, bigger than a birdbath, sat on every table. The wall-to-wall carpet looked a little worn, probably stretched into extra years of service during the war. They might not have joined in the fighting, but Ireland was still on short rations.

I left Wittgenstein in an overstuffed chair and ordered two pints of lager at the bar. The other drinkers sneaked peeks at his rumpled clothes and his frown, and then they turned away. He was a severe-looking man, like a de-frocked priest. He'd have been a good one. I was tempted to confess everything I knew, but I told myself to keep my mouth shut for a while.

The pints sloshed over the rims of the glasses as I carried them from the bar. "Here you go, my friend. I'm not really sure if this is pilsener or lager or just some kind of washed-out ale, but it looks wet." He said *Danke* and we both took a sip. I said, "So what kind of work do you do? Who pays you for thinking about jokes?"

"Cambridge University, I am afraid."

"Really? As in Oxford-and-Cambridge?"

"Yes. I have tricked them into paying me a salary."

We took another sip. I said, "So what do you think about jokes? Or what do you think about when you're thinking about jokes?"

He smiled. "You are demonstrating something important there, Raymond."

"What's that?"

"When you are making jokes, what part of you is making them?"

"My mind, or what's left of it."

"And what part of you is considering my question?"

"That's my mind, too. Maybe some other lobe."

Wittgenstein smiled. "I do not think it is your mind. At least, not as I understand the mind."

"My wife accuses me of thinking with another part of my anatomy." He looked blank. I said, "All right, if I'm not thinking with my mind..."

"It is not thinking. It is being alive to an aspect."

I wondered if he was pulling my leg. "An aspect of what?"

"You must be alive to a certain aspect to make jokes. Or to appreciate music."

I took a long sip of beer. "Ludwig," I said, "I get the feeling that you're saying something important, but I'm only glimpsing a corner of it."

"Do not criticise yourself, Raymond," he said. "The misunderstanding lies in the words. We do not have the words to express it."

"That's decent of you to say, whether it's true or not."

"I know a way to show you. Do you have a pen and a piece of paper?"

I handed him my fountain pen and a white paper napkin. He started sketching something, oblivious to the fusty bar and the holiday drinkers who surrounded us. I sipped at my pint, wondering if the stories I'd heard about him were true.

Wittgenstein turned the napkin around on the table. "What do you see when you look at this?"

I put on my glasses. He had sketched the old rabbit-duck optical illusion. I'd seen more sophisticated renderings of it.

Wittgenstein said, "What do you see?" again. He was itching to tell me the answer, like a kid who knows a riddle.

I said, "It looks like a lopsided French Tickler."

His shoulders slumped, and he looked like somebody had let the air out of him. I tried to meet his big brown eyes, but he was looking at the floor. *Christ*, I thought, *the smartest guy in the world...* I said, "It's a drabbit."

He jumped like somebody had touched him with a live wire. "What did you say, Raymond?"

"It's a drabbit. It could be a *drubbit*, but I like *drabbit* better."

"That is it, Raymond! That is it exactly! A verbal analogue!"

"And if I remember my French, it would be a *clapin*."

"Oh! This is *grossartig*! Do you know what is a *clapier*?"

"Some kind of piano?"

"No, Raymond. It is a rabbit-house!"

He was trembling with excitement. I said, "Can you do it in German?"

"Yes! *Das Kaninchente!*"

That sounded a little labored, but I wasn't going to spoil the fun.

A beefy-looking guy in a plaid shirt stood up from a table on the other side of the room. "Hey!" he said. "Does anybody know the words to *The Stars and Stripes Forever?*"

Somebody said, "You mean *The Star-Spangled Banner?*"

"No! *The Stars and Stripes Forever.* By John Philip Sousa. Dah-*daaah*, da-da-*daaah*, da-da-*daaah*..."

"Oh, yeah. *Be KIND to your WEB-footed FRIENDS...*"

"*That's it! That's it...*"

I said, "Oh, for Christ's sake..."

Wittgenstein snapped out of his reverie. "What is the matter, Raymond?"

"Loud-mouthed Americans get under my skin."

The beefy guy was still standing. "...so since it's the Fourth of July, let's all sing *The Stars and Stripes Forever!* Okay? One, two, three..."

About half of the room joined in.

Be KIND to your WEB-footed FRIENNNNNNDS...

'Cause the DUCK may be SOME-body's MOTHERRRRRRRR...

Who LIVES in a HOUSE by the SWAAAMPPPPP...

Where the WEATHER is DEEP and DAAAMPPPP...

They went on from there with more *Dah-daaah, da-da-daaah, da-da-daaah...* Wittgenstein said, "I know this piece."

The Yanks struggled through the march, and a few of them knew the last line –

...and by their MIGHT, and by the STARS and Stripes for-EVVV-errrrr!

The singers cheered and banged their pints. I started to say that drunks are the same everywhere, but Wittgenstein stood up and said, "Could you sing it again?"

It got very quiet. The beefy man said, "Did I hear you right?"

"Could you sing it again, please? I will accompany you."

The beefy man looked around at the people with him. "Where exactly are you from, pal?"

I was about to put my nickel in, but somebody beat me to it. "Oh, hell, Fred – let's give him another chorus."

Fred started to say *You'd better not be makin' fun of this*, but the others began singing and drowned him out. Halfway through the first phrase – *Be KIND to your WEB-footed FRIENDS* – Wittgenstein started whistling. He sounded exactly like a piccolo, clear and sharp and perfectly tuned. Up and down, like a bird hopping from branch to branch, he wove the counter-melody around the clomp-clomp-clomp of the march. He pushed the singers to keep up with him, and he dazzled them with a trill as they crescendoed to the last line –

...AND BY THEIR MIGHT, AND BY THE STARS AND STRIPES FOREVER!

The whole bar applauded – Irishmen, Yanks, everyone. Fred hurried over, clapped Wittgenstein on the back, and said, "What're you drinking, buddy? Next round's on me!"

Wittgenstein recoiled like a man being groped in a leper colony. "Please don't touch me!"

"Hey, I just wanted to say..."

"Raymond! We must get out of here!"

He headed for the door. While I struggled out of my overstuffed chair, Fred glared at me. "What the hell's the matter with him?"

I said, "Maybe he doesn't like to be glad-handed." I hurried across the bar and into the hall. Wittgenstein had already passed through the lobby, and he was standing on the front steps. I caught up with him, puffing a little.

We stood shoulder to shoulder, looking at the cars in the parking lot. He said, "I don't like those kinds of people."

"I don't like them much either, but..."

"I only wanted to join in the music. Isn't that enough?"

I didn't know what the hell to say. We stood there for a while longer. Wittgenstein said, "Can you take me home, Raymond?"

"I will. In a minute. I have to take a leak first."

Wittgenstein looked at me. "What did you say?"

"I need to use the bathroom. The loo."

"All right. I will wait here."

"Okay." I started to turn away, but my curiosity got the best of me. "How did you learn to whistle like that?"

"I never had to learn," he said. "I always could."

When I got back, Wittgenstein was sitting in a porch-chair, staring into space, drumming his elegant fingers to a rhythm that I couldn't hear. I plopped down beside him. "Ludwig, I thought of a joke that you might appreciate. It's one that most people don't get."

He glared at me. I wondered if I'd offended him, but I plowed ahead. "Heisenberg and Schrödinger are driving down the road, and a cop pulls them over. The cop says, *Do you know how fast you were going?* And Heisenberg says, *No, but I know exactly where we are.*"

Wittgenstein smiled a little, so I went on. "So the cop thinks they're wise-guys, and he decides to inspect he car. He opens the trunk and says, *Hey – do you know you've got a dead cat in here?* And Schrödinger says..."

I looked at Wittgenstein to see if he'd pick up on it. He just looked back at me. I said, "And Schrödinger says, *Well, I do now!*"

He nodded his head and smiled again. "That is very clever, Raymond. Did you make that up yourself?"

"God, no. Somebody told me. But come to think of it, are you here with Schrödinger?"

"What do you mean?"

"I heard that he's here. In Ireland. The President invited him to start up some kind of research center."

"I do not know about that. I am here by myself." He turned away and looked at the porch floor.

I said, "I wonder if he brought his cat," but Wittgenstein didn't seem to think it was funny. I said, "I wish somebody would explain that to me."

"Explain what, Raymond?"

"Explain that business about the cat."

He brightened. "It is a thought-experiment," he said. "You must imagine that you put a cat in a box, along with a piece of uranium and a geiger counter and a capsule of cyanide. If the uranium releases a gamma ray, the geiger counter will detect it, and it will trigger a mechanism that will break open the capsule. You close the lid of the box, and some time passes. Is the cat dead or alive?"

"This is assuming it was alive when you put it in."

"Of course."

I could see that irony wasn't going to get us anywhere. I said, "I've heard the set-up before. But it doesn't make any sense." Wittgenstein looked at me with disapproval, but I went on. "Is Schrödinger alive or dead?"

"I believe he is still alive..."

"Of course he is! And so's Betty Hutton. And so's Harry Truman. And if we want to be sure, we can go back into the hotel and call them up on the phone. If they answer, we know they're alive. Till we hang up, anyway."

"Raymond, you asked me to explain this..."

"I know. Honest to God, I'm not trying to be rude."

Wittgenstein stared at me and took a deep breath. He had a glare that would cut through cast iron. "The point is that in the world of quantum mechanics, two mutually-exclusive states can coexist simultaneously. Then when they are measured, they collapse into one possibility or the other."

"And when Schrödinger opens the box, he gets a faceful of cyanide. Unless he sends his lab assistant..."

"Excuse me," someone said, "but have either of you gentlemen seen a cat?"

The woman standing behind my chair was wearing one of those purple turbans, like rich old dames from the 1930's. She had a Punch-and-Judy kind of face, with a big nose and a prominent chin. She carried herself confidently, like someone who's been well-fed without being pampered. Her perfume made me think of harems and belly-dancers.

"Yes, Madam?" Wittgenstein was on his feet, a model of old-school courtesy, before I could struggle out of my chair.

"I realise that this may seem ridiculous, but he's very dear to me, and expensive, and I'm asking everyone in the hotel. Have you seen him?"

Wittgenstein said, "What kind of cat is he?"

"He's a grey Manx."

Wittgenstein looked at me for help. I said, "They're the kind with the short tails."

"And what is his name?"

"*Aengus.*"

We all looked at each other for a few seconds. I said, "And what is *your* name?"

"Georgie Yeats. But everyone calls me George."

"My God. It's a pleasure to meet you, Mrs Yeats."

"Please call me George. But *have* you seen my cat?"

"I'm afraid not..."

"Raymond," said Wittgenstein, "I know that you are in the oil business, but if you were a writer of detective stories, how would you go about finding a cat?"

"I know what Norbert Davis would do. He'd send his dog to find it."

"Then we must find a dog. We will ask the owner of the hotel."

Oh, Christ, I thought, *there goes my cover.* But Wittgenstein was already escorting Georgie into the lobby.

A serious-looking young guy behind the marble-topped reception desk watched us approach. His name-tag read *Schmidt*. He looked from Georgie Yeats to Wittgenstein to me, wondering what we were up to. Martha St John Gogarty stood behind him, riffling through some file-folders.

I decided to try an end run before they could start. "Martha," I said, "do you have a dog?"

She raised an eyebrow. "You haven't lost my car, have you, Ray?"

"No, but Mrs Yeats here has lost her cat. We need to track it down."

She looked at us the way you'd look at panhandlers on the street. Wittgenstein said, "Your dog can perceive things that we cannot."

Georgie said, "Would you mind terribly, Neenie?"

She shook her head, more exasperated than defeated. "Klaus," she said to the young guy, "would you mind bringing Tully around from the kennel? I'll watch the desk."

Klaus cocked an eyebrow of his own, but he said, "*Ja, Madame*," and hurried across the lobby. Wittgenstein and I looked at each other. Georgie drew Martha into a rambling chat about how she appreciated everything, and how much her cat meant to her, and how she had such fond memories of the old Renvyle House. Martha looked like she wished that we'd all checked into a different hotel.

Klaus came through the front door with an Irish wolfhound on a leash. The dog stood over three feet tall, with shaggy grey hair and psychotic yellow eyes. If it reared up on its hind legs, it would have been taller than any of us. It sniffed my knuckles, and I scratched it behind the ears. It swung its big head over to inspect Wittgenstein, but he stepped back out of range.

"Tully!" said Martha Gogarty. "Sit!" The big creature lowered its hindquarters onto the floor, grinning a slobbery grin and looking for approval.

"Is he any good at tracking?" I asked.

"You said you wanted to borrow a dog, Raymond," said Martha. "You didn't specify a bloodhound."

"He'll be fine." I took the leash from Klaus. "Ludwig, could you hold him for a minute?"

Wittgenstein took the leash, holding it away from his side like a live rattlesnake. I said, "Now, Georgie – we need something that smells like your cat."

She rummaged in her purse and pulled out a brush. "I groom Aengus with this."

"That's perfect." I held the brush in front of Tully's nose. He sniffed it with mild interest and flopped his head down on the floor.

"Do you think he understands?" asked Wittgenstein.

Georgie Yeats said, "Give me the brush." She knelt down beside the dog, looking it in the eye. "Listen, Tully," she crooned, "This is from my cat. I've lost my cat, and I miss him. I need you to help find him. Can you do that for me?"

Tully took a deep breath and clambered up onto his feet. Wittgenstein said, "Would you hold him please, Raymond?"

I took the leash. Klaus went back behind the desk, exchanging eye-rolling glances with Martha – *What the hell are these people up to, anyway?* – and they both returned to their bookkeeping. I gave Tully a scratch behind the ears and patted his flanks. "So, Georgie," I said, "where was the last place you saw your cat?"

"I took a seaweed bath this morning," she said. "He was with me down there."

"You took him into the bathtub with you?"

"No, of course not! But I took him down to that wing."

"Didn't you lock him in your room?"

"I wouldn't do that to Aengus. Besides, he might tear up my dressing gown."

I looked her over. She wasn't a bad-looking woman, and I sensed a possibility. I couldn't tell if she was interested, or if she was one of those women who always left a lure hanging over the side of the boat. I said, "So where are the baths?"

She said, "I'll show you," and headed down the hall into the center of the hotel.

Wittgenstein and I followed Georgie through a maze of corridors, with Tully tagging along at an amiable pace. I said, "Georgie, you have a nice touch with the dog."

"I can read him," she said.

We walked a few steps more. Wittgenstein said, "What else can you read, Mrs Yeats?"

She looked around the corridor with its flocked wallpaper and dark woodwork. "I can still read the old hotel," she said. "The one that burned down."

"Was it here? In this place?"

"It was at the back of the property. Where the seaweed baths are now."

"I've got to ask," I said. " *What* did you read in the old hotel?"

Georgie drew herself up and walked with a little swagger. "There was a ghost."

Wittgenstein didn't say anything. I said, "I suppose that most old Irish houses have their ghosts…"

"His name was Athelstone Blake," she said. "I saw his face in a mirror."

We rounded a corner and walked up a flight of stairs. Georgie said, "He had died when he was fourteen. He moved furniture and threw things. When Willy and I were here, they had to send someone up to take the door off the hinges. He had blocked it shut with a linen chest."

Wittgenstein said, "When were you here?"

"Thirty years ago. On our honeymoon."

I didn't say anything. I'd heard stories about the Yeats honeymoon. Wittgenstein said, "After you saw the ghost in the mirror..."

"I saw him twice, actually. Even after they moved the furniture away from the door, we kept hearing sobs and murmurs from the room. So I went back to investigate."

"You and your husband?"

"No, I went by myself."

Wittgenstein and I waited while she drew out the moment theatrically. Finally I said, "What did you see."

"I saw a boy with red hair. He looked like he'd seen things that no boy should ever see." We waited until she went on. "He said that he didn't like people living in his house."

"Did you say anything to him?"

"I told him that I was sorry that his life was so short, but that it wasn't right for him to frighten other people. I asked him what he'd like – what would make him feel better."

"And he said..."

"He asked for incense. And flowers. So that's what we put in his room. And he never bothered anyone after that."

I almost tripped over the dog. He had turned in front of me, and he was standing sideways in the corridor, sniffing at the bottom of the door. I said, "What have you got, Tully? Is the cat in there?"

Georgie smiled at me. "I'm beginning to have more confidence as we go along."

"What do you mean?"

"That's my room. He smells Aengus."

Wittgenstein said, "Are you sure that he is not in there, Mrs Yeats?"

"I'm positive, but – oh, here, see for yourselves."

She took a key from a coat pocket and opened the door. Georgie had a fancier room than mine – a writing desk and an ornamental iron table with a spray of red roses in a vase, plus a huge double bed. Heavy doors led to a dressing-room and a bathroom, and a big mullioned window looked out toward the sea. Tully snuffled under the bed. Wittgenstein got down on his knees, looked from the other side of the bed and said, "There is nothing here."

"I'm afraid this is going to be a problem," I said. "This dog thinks he's found the cat. If we drag him out of here, he's going to want to come back in."

"Let me have him," said Georgie. I handed her the leash. "Come here, Tully. We need to talk." The dog followed her into the dressing-room, and she shut the door.

Wittgenstein stared at me and said, "I have realised something."

"What?"

"You are Doan."

"What?"

"I saw it when you took the leash. The dog is like Carstairs, and you are like Doan. You *are* Doan."

I felt that hot flush again. "I don't know what you're talking about."

"I remember exactly how Norbert Davis describes him, Raymond. *He was short and a little on the plump side, and he had a chubby, pink face and a smile as innocent and appealing as a baby's. He looked like a nice, pleasant sort of person, and on rare occasions he was.*"

I said, "I'm not sure I'm flattered by that."

Wittgenstein looked surprised. "Surely you cannot be offended by a metaphor."

"Why not? A good metaphor is a punch in the guts." We stood there for a few seconds in silence. Wittgenstein looked like a kid who'd had his knuckles rapped. I said, "I've never cared much for Doan. He's a brute. If he didn't have the dog..."

The dressing-room door opened, and Tully walked out. Georgie handed me the leash. "We can go now," she said. "He understands."

Tully led us down a flight of stairs to another ground-level corridor. Wittgenstein said, "Where are we, exactly?"

Georgie was trotting ahead, full of herself. "We're almost there."

We turned a corner and saw a sign over a door that read *Seaweed Baths*. There was a tall glass window in the door, and someone had painted a mermaid on the glass. She was reclining in an old-fashioned bathtub with her hair draped over her breasts and her tail hanging over the side of the tub. Tully whined and tugged on the leash. We stepped through the door into a steamy room with benches along the walls and a grid of wooden planks underfoot. I could see a tile floor through the spaces between the planks, and it looked wet. A chubby girl sat behind a desk in front of a wall of numbered hooks. A wicker basket beside the desk was half-filled with damp towels, and clean towels were stacked on the shelves behind her. The girl looked up from a magazine on the desk with a slightly-alarmed expression and said, "You can't bring a dog – oh, hello, Mrs Yeats."

"Hello, Clodagh. I was hoping you'd still be here."

I was falling in love with Irish women's names. *Cloe-dah*. The girl said, "I've looked everywhere for your cat, Mrs Yeats. I'm sure he isn't here."

"Yes, thank you, I'm sure you have. You don't mind if we have another nosey around, do you?"

She looked dubiously at Tully. "Mister Vertsag said that I wasn't to let any animals in here..."

I said, "What about Mrs Yeats's cat?"

"Well, I thought – after all, it was just a cat..."

Wittgenstein said, "What is the name of the man who gave you those instructions?"

"Mister Vertsag. He's the manager of the hotel."

I said, "You don't mean that German kid at the front desk, do you?"

"Oh, no. Mister Vertsag is older. Like you."

Georgie said, "I asked Martha Gogarty to let me bring Aengus in here as a favour." I could almost hear the *u* as she spoke. "I haven't gotten you into trouble, have I, dear?"

Tully pulled at the leash. I said, "Our friend seems to think that your cat is still here. Did you take him into the bath with you, Georgie?"

"He was with me when I was changing, but I think he slipped out when Clodagh brought in the towels."

I looked at Clodagh. "Do you usually..."

"I had to get extras from the storeroom," she said. "We were out of them this morning. I brought them down to Mrs Yeats."

"Okay." I turned to Georgie. "What room were you in?"

Georgie looked at Clodagh, and Clodagh looked at a logbook. "You were in Eight."

I said, "Can we go in there?"

Clodagh said, "That would be fine. There's no one in there right now. But I should stay here at the desk."

Georgie led us down a hallway with more wooden planks over another wet tiled floor. Tully pulled and strained at the leash, and I planted my feet firmly to make sure I didn't slip. Wittgenstein brought up the rear, trying to get my attention. "Raymond..."

"Just a minute..."

"We must talk to this manager..."

"Hang on, Ludwig. I don't want to fall on my butt."

Georgie opened a door with a large numeral *8* on a plaque. The room was about ten feet square, with another grid of wooden planks over the tiled floor. There were pegs in the walls for hanging clothes. A plywood box with a hinged lid and a hole in the top sat in the corner. But the room was dwarfed by the bathtub – an extra-long claw-foot tub with huge taps. Water pipes ran up the wall, and everything was covered with multiple coats of thick white paint.

I said, "Christ, this looks like a setup for one of Agatha's stories." Wittgenstein said, "*Marienbad.*"

Tully tried to pull me back out into the hall. I said, "Georgie, are you sure the cat's not in that steam bath?"

Georgie said, "I looked in here before," but she opened the lid on the plywood box. "There's nothing but a stool."

"Okay. Let's follow the dog."

Tully led us to the end of the corridor, and he sniffed at the bottom of the door on the left. The plaque read *13*. A hand-lettered sign was pinned on the doorframe with a tack. *Out of Order.*

I pushed at the door, but it didn't move. I had to give it a hard shove before it yielded. The hinges groaned as it swung open. Tully bounded into the room and put his paws up on the side of the tub.

The cat was lying near the drain, tangled in a mass of wet green seaweed. Georgie shrieked and pushed past me to lift it out. The cat lolled back and forth in her hands like a rag doll. She shook the limp creature. "Aengus! Oh, my God! What happened?"

Wittgenstein and I looked at each other. Footsteps came pounding down the wooden walkway in the hall, and Clodagh stuck her head into the room. "What's the matter?"

"He's dead! How could you let this happen?"

"What was he doing in here?"

"What were *you* doing? You're supposed to be in charge here..."

"Mrs Yeats," said Wittgenstein, "I think his feet are moving."

Georgie held the cat at arm's length. "My God, you're right. Clodagh! Get a vet!"

Clodagh ran back to her desk and Georgie stumbled after her, cradling the cat in her arms. We could hear Clodagh's voice, frantic but indistinct, as she phoned the front desk. She put the receiver down with a clatter, and the two women ran out of the seaweed baths.

There was a hint of a sweet odor in the air that I couldn't place – not perfume, not food. I looked at the tub. The rubber stopper dangled from a chain that was looped around the spigot. I said, "I guess this is poetic justice."

"What do you mean, Raymond?"

"I always thought that locked-room mysteries were ridiculous. Now I've stumbled into one."

Wittgenstein said, "I have thought about locked rooms, too."

Chapter Three

"You don't have a shot of bourbon, do you?"

"I'm afraid not, Raymond. Could I offer you some tea?"

"Okay. Tea."

Wittgenstein's cottage looked like a cell in a bankrupt monastery. We were sitting on mismatched chairs at a wooden table. The sun was still shining outside, but the gloom in his one-room cubicle was thick enough to cut with a knife. Wittgenstein filled a teakettle from a tap at the sink and then struggled with a box of damp matches to light a gas-ring. He extracted two mugs from a pile of dirty dishes and rinsed them under the tap. I hoped that the tea-water would be hot enough to kill whatever might be growing in them.

The table was covered with papers and notebooks. More books and papers sat in lopsided stacks on the floor. I looked at an open notebook by my elbow. The pages were thick with writing and marginal notes, and some sentences had been obliterated by furious scribbling. It was mostly in German, with occasional phrases in English. I fought an impulse to turn the pages.

Two birds flapped at the window over the sink. Wittgenstein took a piece of bread from a drawer, tore it into small pieces, and opened the window. He held the handful of crumbs over the ledge, and the birds pecked the food from his palm. They were small and brown, with reddish breasts and faces.

"Francis of Assisi," I said.

"Do not canonise me, Raymond. I have enough trouble being human."

"Don't we all? How did you get them to eat out of your hand?"

"I offered bread to them every day for a month before they would trust me."

I decided against asking *why* and said, "What kind of birds are those?"

"They are robins."

"Robins? They're scrawnier than their American cousins..."

"They are *Rotkehlchen*. Excuse me for a moment, Raymond." Wittgenstein brushed the breadcrumbs from his hands, poured two cups of tea, and sat at the table. He started writing in a notebook. I kept thinking about Georgie Yeats running out of the seaweed baths with the limp cat in her arms. She must have run all the way to the lobby, because by the time Wittgenstein and I got there with the dog, she and Martha Gogarty had gone. Klaus told us that they'd gone off in Martha's car – her other car, a beat-up Renault – to find a vet. I'd handed him the dog's leash, and he'd acted as sniffy as ever. It still raised my hackles to think about him, even back in Wittgenstein's cottage. Hotel clerks and headwaiters – snooty sons of bitches who made a living by looking down their noses at everybody else.

But I kept thinking about Georgie Yeats while I sipped my tea. She wore old clothes, the baggy kind that hadn't been in fashion since the Twenties, but there were womanly curves under there. I knew that she was twenty-five years younger than Yeats when they got married. And Yeats had been dead since 1939.

I said, "It doesn't make any sense…"

"Just one moment, Raymond." Wittgenstein kept writing. I walked around the room, lit a cigarette, stubbed it out and threw it into the fireplace. I wanted to talk. "Now," he said, putting down his pen. "What were you saying?"

"Have you ever owned a cat, Ludwig?"

"My mother had them. I think that it is cruel to keep animals in captivity."

"I have one at home. She's a mean old puss, and she won't let anybody touch her. Most of the time she ignores me, but once in a while she'll bring me a live mouse for a present."

Wittgenstein smiled. "I would be reluctant to ascribe motives to her, Raymond. If she could speak, we would not be able to understand her."

"One thing I do understand is that she hates water. She wouldn't go near a bathtub unless you threw her in there. And if you did, she'd take half of your arm along with her."

"And so you think that it is unlikely…"

"Yes, to say the least. The only way that cat would have ended up in the tub would be if somebody had intentionally tried to kill it."

"But if that were the case, why would they pull the stopper?"

"That's exactly what doesn't make sense. Could they be trying to make it look like an accident?"

"Perhaps in fact it *was* an accident?"

"You sound like my wife," I said. "She tells me I have too much imagination. I don't think I've got enough."

"It was very slippery in there…"

"But what's the sequence of events? Somebody is in there taking a seaweed bath. They pull the plug and leave. Then the cat goes in, jumps up onto the rim of the tub and falls in."

Wittgenstein started writing something else. I realized he was one of those people who'd never pay full attention to what you were saying, even if he was looking at you. He reminded me of Billy Wilder. I said, "The cat had to fall in at just the right time – while there was still enough water in the tub to drown in. And it had to be a cat that couldn't swim."

"But it did not drown, Raymond..."

"I'll get to that in a minute. The door stuck a little. Somebody had to pull it shut."

"So you believe..."

"I'll tell you what I don't believe. I don't believe that someone got out of the bathtub, pulled the plug, put on some clothes – at least a bathrobe – and then opened the door long enough for a cat to get in. Then they shut the door without noticing the cat, and the cat jumped up on the rim of the tub and fell in."

"It is not impossible."

"I don't buy it. Too many *if*s. I think that somebody deliberately tried to kill that cat."

"Why would someone want to do that?"

"Christ, I don't know. Spite? Pure meanness? Why do kids pull the wings off flies?" We sat there and looked at each other. I said, "If we go back over to the hotel and look at the sign-in sheet for the baths..."

"I think it may require a deeper investigation than that, Raymond."

I looked at the rumpled, unshaven little guy and said, "Yeah? What?"

"I have been writing about investigations. Do you speak German?"

"A little. Not enough. No."

"I will translate." He turned to a page in his notebook. "*People who have never carried out an investigation of a philosophical sort are not equipped with the right optical instruments for that sort of investigation or scrutiny.*"

He looked up at me. I said, "Is there more?"

"Yes. *Someone who is not used to searching in the forest for berries will not find any because his eye has not been sharpened for such things, and he does not know where you have to be particularly on the lookout for them. Similarly, someone unpractised in philosophy passes by all the spots where difficulties lie hidden under the grass, while someone with practice pauses and senses that there is a difficulty here, even though he does not yet see it...*"

"I guess that's usually true..."

"*...and no wonder, if one knows how long even the practised investigator, who realises there is a difficulty, has to search in order to find it.*"

He looked up, waiting for me to say something. I said, "So we're launching a philosophical investigation of a wet cat?"

He looked down at the floor, but then he started to laugh. "You are right, Raymond. I am constructing a foundation to hold up a feather. That is why I like *Street and Smith's Detective Magazine.* I like to hear pretences being deflated."

"I always liked *Black Mask* better. And they pay better."

Wittgenstein's eyes lit up. "How would you know that, Raymond?"

"I read it someplace. But what about the cat?"

"Yes, the cat. I have been thinking about locked-room mysteries..."

"I thought that philosophers thought about the meaning of life."

"That is what I keep trying to argue. Or more precisely, I point out that they waste their time addressing the linguistic – *Knoten?* – that they keep creating for themselves. What is the word?"

"Knots?"

"No, that is too orderly. I mean – *Gewirr?*"

"Tangles? You won't get any argument from me if that's what you mean. So what do you think philosophers are supposed to do?"

"A philosopher should uncover pieces of plain nonsense. And he should display the bumps that he has got by running his head up against the limits. His bumps make us see the value of his discovery."

"I'd rather have the discovery without the bumps. But I thought we were talking about locked rooms."

"We are. And I have written about it." Wittgenstein flipped through a notebook. "Here – *Ein Mensch ist in einem Zimmer gefangen...*"

"Ludwig, my German isn't up to this."

"Of course, Raymond. So – *Someone is imprisoned in a room if the door is unlocked...*"

"Wait a minute..."

"*...and it opens inwards; but it doesn't occur to him to pull, rather than push against it.*"

I fiddled with a cigarette but decided not to light it. I thought *There must be an easier way to say that*, but I didn't want it to sound like an insult. I said, "So the room isn't locked. But somebody put a *Push* sign where it ought to say *Pull*."

"Yes! That is my point exactly!"

"And your job is to switch the signs?"

"It is more complicated than that. I am trying to show the fly the way out of the fly-bottle."

"Okay. But the cat couldn't read. And it wasn't strong enough to push or pull. And the door was stuck."

"Mister Wittgenstein?" A man was standing at the door of the cottage.

"Tommy! I am glad to see you. Do you have any bourbon for my friend Raymond?"

The man looked at me dubiously. He was short and jowly, with a shock of curly grey hair that hadn't been cut for a while. "I think Herself might have some *poitín* back at the house..."

I said, "Thanks, but don't bother," and he looked relieved. He turned back to Wittgenstein and held out a glass jar. "She sent this over for you." It looked like broth. "She says you need to eat something besides them biscuits."

Wittgenstein took the jar and set it on the floor by the sink. "Please thank her for me. I am sorry that I do not have anything to offer in return."

"She said she'd come over and clean up for you in here..."

"No! I cannot have anyone cleaning here until I finish writing." We all looked around the clutter-strewn room. Wittgenstein said, "Tell her that I will notify her when I am done."

Tommy shook his head. "She told me to ask – do you need any messages?"

"No, Tommy. Thank you."

"She said for me to tell you – all that tinned food will be the death of you."

"Tell her not to worry, Tommy. People live too long anyway."

He shrugged and walked out the door. We listened to his footsteps crunching on the gravel as he walked up the path. I said, "Messages? From Cambridge?"

Wittgenstein looked puzzled. "Are you making a joke, Raymond?"

"I wasn't making a joke. I was asking a question. What messages was he talking about?"

"When Tommy speaks of messages, he means groceries."

I shook my head. "It's going to take me a while to understand Irish, or whatever kind of English they speak over here."

"Yes. We are engaged in a struggle with language."

"For a while I thought I was going to have to learn French again. If you have a toilet in your hotel room, that's *en suite*."

Wittgenstein smiled. "Sometimes you have to take an expression out of the language, to send it for cleaning. Then you can put it back into circulation."

"That's a good idea, Ludwig. I wish more editors thought like that. But how on earth did they get from *groceries* to *messages*?"

"I have no idea, Raymond. But I must perform an investigation."

"Are you talking about the cat again?"

"I am talking about the manager of the hotel."

"What about him?"

"His name is Vertsag."

"So?"

Wittgenstein drew a row of *X*'s on a piece of paper. "I knew of a man named Vertsag during the war."

"Which war?"

"I was in the Austrian Army in the Great War. In 1918."

"In Intelligence?"

"No, I was in the trenches. I was not going to sit in a tent behind the lines while other men were dying. Do you know how that would feel?"

I thought about that for a minute. "I was in that war, too. In France. Where were you stationed?"

"On the Russian Front."

We both felt relieved. I said, "So what did they have you doing out there?"

"That is what I want to tell you about. I was in an observation post, on the front line. My job was to report the details of the skirmishes, and the casualties."

"We had observers, too. A lot of them got killed because they were too busy writing to shoot back."

Wittgenstein said, "I saw Vertsag in a place called Ldziany. It was sunset, and the guns had stopped firing. I remember because it was getting dark, and I was having trouble seeing the paper that I was writing on."

"And you weren't about to light a lamp..."

Wittgenstein shook his head. "There was still enough light for me to see across No-Man's-Land. Both sides had mounted assaults during the day, and both had been repelled with machine-gun fire. There were dozens of men lying in the mud. Dead and wounded."

"I remember. I saw the same kind of thing."

"Everyone was waiting for the light to fade. I was writing when I heard the pistol-fire. Then I saw Lieutenant Vertsag."

"Was he from your battalion?"

"No. I do not know where he came from. But he was walking slowly, wearing his officer's coat, and making no attempt to shield himself. He had a pistol in his hand. He walked from one body to another, executing the wounded men. Shooting them in the head."

"You mean the Russians?"

"No. He was shooting *all* of the wounded men. Austrians too. I could hear them pleading with him before he shot them."

"Why didn't somebody shoot him?"

"Why does anyone do anything on a battlefield, Raymond? Why do they not do the sane thing and run away?" He glared at me. "We all sat and watched that man walk through the mud and the barbed wire. He reloaded his pistol and shot the wounded men until he ran out of ammunition. Then he walked away."

We sat there for a while, listening to the waves lapping on the concrete pier outside the cottage. I said, "Did you find out who he was?"

"I asked when I turned in my report that night, but my commanding officer would not tell me. I had to ask the men. They said that Lieutenant Vertsag was a legend on the Eastern Front. But no one knew where he was stationed, or where he could be found."

"Maybe it wasn't just one man. Maybe this was something that different officers did…"

Wittgenstein wasn't listening to me. He said, "I wrote about the killings in my report, but when I went to the files a week later, that part had been deleted."

"Could they have been mercy killings? Putting the badly-wounded ones out of their misery?"

"I don't think so, Raymond. He wasn't stopping to look."

"So you think that the hotel manager could be…"

"It is an unusual name. I must speak to him and find out."

"If he's the officer who liked to execute wounded soldiers, he might get nasty if someone tries to nose around in his past."

"Then I might get a bump on the head. But now you must excuse me, Raymond. I have a thought that I must capture." He picked up the pen and started writing again.

I stepped out of the cottage and walked along the wide concrete dock. A mangy cat prowled around a pile of lobster-pots. A boat was loosely tethered to a vertical iron pipe on the side of the dock so that it could slide up and down with the tides. It looked like a cartoon tugboat, with tires hanging over both sides. Or *tyres*, I reminded myself. I knew it was pronounced the same way, but the spelling made me think of Jeeves and Bertie Wooster. *My good man, we seem to have punctured our tyres.*

The sun was still high in the sky. I liked thinking about the whole business of daylight in northern latitudes. I knew that Ireland was as far north as Labrador because I'd looked it up. The further north you went, the longer the summer evenings would be. Beyond the Arctic Circle, the sun would stay above the horizon all night. And in the winter it wouldn't come up at all.

In a field across the bay, an old manor house had fallen into ruin. The windows were broken, and sheep grazed the un-mowed grounds. It was a big boxy house, like the one that belonged to my mother's family in Waterford. I wondered if the Thorntons still lived there. They were a cold crew – Anglo-Irish Quakers who looked down their noses at the rest of the human race. God's Frozen People. I could see why my mother had left them to live in America, and it must have been galling for her to come back, flat-broke and divorced, with a seven-year-old son. Her mother and sisters spent days without speaking to us, but they dragged us to their Quaker Meetings. Isolated souls sitting on hard benches with their eyes half-shut. They called it The Silence. I wondered if they were soaring in spiritual ecstasy or just cat-napping.

My mother must have begged her lawyer-brother to get us away from Waterford. He moved us to a house that he owned in London, and then he paid my tuition at Dulwich College. I became the American kid from the Irish family who got stuck into an English boys' school. No wonder I've never known who the hell I am.

Wittgenstein stuck his head out of the cottage door. "I am finished now, Raymond."

I said, "How did you find this place?"

"It belongs to my friend Con Drury. I visited here before the war. It is a perfect place to think."

"I suppose – if you like to think in cold, dark places."

"But that is exactly it, Raymond. Everywhere else is under – *das grelle?* – under the electric lights. I truly believe they generate a force-field that interferes with our thinking."

"If you believe that, don't ever come to California. They've just about outlawed darkness there."

"I have no interest…" Wittgenstein shook his head. "No, I would rather be here. I can only think when it is dark. This is the last pool of darkness in Europe."

We heard another crunch of boots on gravel, and a man appeared on the hillside path behind the cottage. He had a bowlegged, rolling gait, like somebody who'd had rickets as a kid. He walked past without looking at us, scowling like a guard dog. He climbed aboard the fishing boat, opened a hatch in the afterdeck and lowered himself into it. I said, "Friendly neighbors, hmm?"

"He is a Carney. They live behind the hill."

"Do they visit you? Like Tommy?"

"No, not at all. They told me to stay off their land. They said I am frightening their sheep."

Carney emerged from the hatch and untied the mooring-lines. He unlocked the door of the small wooden cabin and stepped inside. The engine roared into life, shooting a cloud of dark soot out of a smokestack. I said, "That can't be good for thinking."

Wittgenstein shouted, "What?"

"That noise can't be good for thinking! How often does this happen?"

"Every day or two! Sometimes in the middle of the night!"

The engine roared and the boat eased away from the dock, leaving us in a cloud of oily smoke. I said, "Noisy neighbors, no electricity – nice place you've got here."

Wittgenstein shrugged. "I prefer it to Cambridge."

I drove back toward the hotel, checking my watch against the clock in the car. It was eight o'clock in the evening, but it felt earlier. The sun hurt my eyes as I followed the narrow road to the west, and I wished I'd brought a pair of sunglasses.

I pulled over to a wide spot – a *lay-by*, the Irish called it – to avoid a flock of sheep in the middle of the road. A wizened farmer wearing one of those flat-caps herded the sheep with a long stick, and they flowed around the car while a frisky border collie chased the strays. I wondered what it would be like to live in a flock, a pack, a swarm. It would take a set of instincts that I couldn't imagine. No, I was a loner. I'd never run with a herd.

I lit a cigarette. It was a relief to get away from Wittgenstein. He wanted – what? He wanted to talk. He wanted to be understood, but he could be damned difficult to understand. Was his German as confusing as his English? I suspected it was. He used too many abstractions. Why did so many smart people talk in a cloud of abstractions?

Mostly he was lonely. I could feel it a mile away. It was in his posture, his scruffy clothes – and in the way he spoke, like a recently-arrived immigrant trying to communicate out of a phrase book. It was in those deep-set eyes, and the way he stared – until you looked back at him, and then he'd look over your shoulder, into some middle distance that only he could see. He acted like he was trapped in a cage of glass, hoping that someone would come along with a hammer and smash it. I knew what that felt like, because I felt that way most of the time.

Usually I blamed it on America. I'd lived in Los Angeles for thirty-six years, minus two years in the trenches in France, and I still felt like a beggar at the feast. It didn't matter who I was with, or what we talked about. I got along with the postman well enough, or with the guy at the grocery store. But put me into a room with a bunch of salesmen, or Hollywood hot-shots, and I'd repel them like a cross-wired magnet. The same thing would happen with university types – two minutes into a conversation, and they'd start looking around for someone else to talk to. And then there were the rich. Talking to them was like trying to climb naked up the side of a glacier.

Except for Warren Lloyd. When I'd sailed from Southampton to the US in 1912, I found myself in an assigned seat at a dinner table with the Lloyd family – Warren with his Yale law degree, Alma with her sculpture and poetry. They'd taken two of their children on an American version of the Grand Tour, boring Estelle and Edward with tours of stately homes and museums but trying to make it up to them with horseback rides and climbing expeditions and other forms of money-fuelled enthusiasm. Estelle had tolerated the trip without much interest until I sat down across the starched linen of the circular table, exotic as Mister D'Arcy in my blazer and white ducks, and speaking with an accent that stole her fourteen-year-old heart. "Say *Worcestershire*," she'd beg me. "Say *Strawberry*."

Warren and I shared a fascination with chess. We spent the sunny afternoons on the promenade deck and the rainy ones in the bar, setting up classic chess problems from a book in the shipboard library and trying odd gambits to see if we could find better solutions. When we played against each other, he consistently clobbered me. Whether he played white or black, he'd seize an early advantage and push me remorselessly into one lopsided exchange after another. Estelle would curl up with a book in a nearby deck chair, pretending to read.

When we docked in New York, the Lloyds urged me to move to Los Angeles, but I had a headful of romantic ideas about freebooting my way across America. Forty-eight hours later, I wished I'd taken the train with them. Most of the Americans I met pretended to be too busy to talk, and they had nothing to say when they did. Most of them wanted to write me off with a quick label –

Limey, huh? – but a few looked me over like a horse at an auction, wondering if they could use me to make a buck.

I worked at day-labor jobs, selling myself too cheap. I picked apricots and strung tennis rackets. The £500 that I'd borrowed from my Irish uncle began to dwindle, with no prospect of finding a steady job. I'd told him that I'd take my mother off his hands after I got established, but on the lousy wages I was earning I couldn't even support myself.

While I wandered from New Orleans to Seattle to San Francisco, I sent postcards to the Lloyds, usually with limericks –

> *A fellow named Chandler strings rackets*
> *And resides in the low-income brackets*
>   *It seems education*
>   *Means zilch in this nation*
> *Without the connections to back it.*

And everywhere I went, I saw the ads in the newspapers: *California: The Italy of America. Twelve Months of Sunshine. The Healthiest Climate in the World.*

It took me a year to swallow my pride. Warren welcomed me like an old and erring friend – a Prodigal Younger Brother, a kindred spirit. *Whose butt was I supposed to kick on the chessboard when you weren't around?* I'd barely settled into their guest-room before he arranged an interview for me at a Los Angeles creamery – a perfunctory chat that concluded with a job offer and a handshake. *Any friend of Warren's is a friend of mine.*

I threw the cigarette out the window – no need to worry about a California brush-fire in this soggy place – and restarted the car, steering around an ancient woman on a bicycle. I wondered what Wittgenstein was doing. Probably scratching away in his notebooks, nibbling on biscuits, forgetting the broth that Tommy's wife had sent over. I was glad that he hadn't asked me to stay for dinner. I wanted beef and potatoes and a good Irish beer to wash it all down. The Renvyle House kitchen hadn't disappointed me yet.

But Wittgenstein – what was it about him? I'd never read anything he'd written – reading philosophy gave me a headache when I tried – but I'd heard stories about him. How the university students would fight to get into his classes, and then he'd sit in front of them for hours without saying a word. How he'd storm out of a room if he thought that someone wasn't paying attention.

And I'd heard a story about how he'd taken a woman to Norway. She must have thought that it was going to be the start of something special – a romantic getaway with one of the rich Wittgensteins – but he'd parked her in a hotel and gone off to a cabin in the woods to pray. After she got over being disappointed, she got bored, and then she got mad. After a few days she took herself back home. I wondered if Wittgenstein just forgot about her. He didn't seem to be much of a ladies' man.

I pulled into the Renvyle House parking lot, but I didn't get out of the car. A clammy speculation had wormed itself into my guts, and I couldn't push it away. Had I been batting my eyelashes at him? I hadn't worried myself into that kind of misery since I'd known Cissy. I felt like I was twenty-five again – lonely, hungry for human contact, but unable to tell a handshake of friendship from a grope of lust. And what the hell did I want, anyway? I hadn't known then, and I still didn't.

A man in a brown topcoat knocked at the window of the car. He was a tall, clean-shaven guy with pale blue eyes behind wire-rimmed glasses. He wore a snap-brim grey hat. He looked like an Army officer in civvies, or a tax man. I detested tax men.

I rolled down the window and looked at him. He said, "Chandler?"

"Who the hell are you?"

"Name's Bocklett. O.S.S."

He had a flat American accent, from somewhere out in the midwest. I said, "I've heard of you."

He pulled back a little. "You couldn't have."

"Not you personally. The Office of Strategic Services. The dirty-tricks guys."

He looked me over. "You were in the Army, weren't you?"

"That's so long ago I don't even remember."

He sneered. "We saved a lot of you Army guys from getting shot."

"You weren't around when I was in the Army. And I wasn't in your Army." I got out of the car and turned around to lock it.

He said, "It'll be better if we talk out here. Where we can have some privacy."

"Who said I want to talk?"

"You're on a HUAC list."

I stopped and turned around. He was a beefy specimen under the topcoat, and he knew how to radiate a threat. I said, "Okay. Let's sit in the car."

"Smoke?"

He said, "No," and rolled down the window. We looked out at the parking lot for a while. Bocklett ran a finger across the rosewood dashboard. He looked like he could sit there all day.

I said, "Okay. Let's hear what you've got. And if you've got a subpoena, I want to see it."

He seemed to be chewing over a thought. He looked around at the upholstered interior of the car. Finally he said, "Are you writing a book over here?"

"Hold it. You don't know who I am..."

"Yes, I do. And you're on the Soft List."

"And what the hell does that mean?"

"It means that they're thinking about calling you in to testify."

"About what, for Christ's sake?"

Bocklett shrugged. "They'll want to know the names of people you've worked with. And who you went to meetings with."

"Then they wouldn't get much out of me. I work on my own. And I hate meetings."

"But you wrote that, didn't you?" He looked around at the copy of *The High Window* lying on the back seat.

"If I did – and I'm not saying that I did – so what? It's just a detective story."

"There's a reference to a John Reed Club."

He'd done his homework. I said, "So maybe they ought to subpoena Philip Marlowe."

He turned and looked at me. His eyes were as cold as a snake's. "Don't smart off to the Committee. The smartasses end up in jail."

I shook my head. "I know. The Hollywood Ten. A sorry bunch of neurotics with lousy marriages and a taste for booze..."

"And they were convicted..."

"That isn't hard when there's nobody to defend them. The studio bosses paid those guys peanuts, and then they dropped them like hot potatoes when HUAC stuck their noses in the door."

We sat there for a while. I threw my cigarette out the window and said, "So they sent you all the way over here to threaten me?"

"I don't work for HUAC. But Army Intelligence gets briefed, and they brief us."

"So why are you telling me this?"

"I thought you'd appreciate it if somebody told you."

"I'd appreciate it if you'd leave me the hell alone."

He turned to me and looked again through those wire-rimmed glasses with a cop's steady gaze. "So what brings you to Ireland?"

I thought about saying *I came here for the waters*, but enough was enough. "Tell them I'm here for personal reasons. Nobody's business but mine."

"You planning to stay around here?" He reached for the door handle.

"That depends," I said. "What are *you* doing here, anyway?"

He looked out the front window for a second before he said, "Fishing, Take care of yourself, Chandler." He stepped out of the car and walked into the hotel. I waited until he was out of sight before I moved.

Klaus was still at the front desk. Through an open door behind him, I could see Martha Gogarty sitting at a desk. She glanced up from whatever she was working on, and I caught her eye. I said, "I need to talk with you. In private."

She waved me in. Klaus gave me a dirty look as I walked around the end of the counter, brushed past him, and closed the door of Martha's office behind me. She made a little show out of putting the cap back on her fountain pen. "What do you want now, Ray?"

"Absolutely nothing. But I thought we had an understanding. I came here for peace and quiet and privacy."

"Privacy?" She raised an eyebrow. "Is that why you borrowed my dog and marched through the lobby and searched the hotel for George Yeats's cat?"

"Okay. You have a point. But everybody seems to know who I am."

"You're not exactly an anonymous citizen, Ray. Your photo is on every one of your books."

"Is that why people keep coming up to me and asking..."

"What do you want me to do? I've registered you as Ray Thornton, and I could get into trouble for doing that. I'm letting you drive my car..."

"And I appreciate that." I started to pull out a cigarette, but I stopped myself. I said, "Look, Martha. My nerves are shot. I'm not trying to be an ingrate, but..."

She shook her head. "Don't torture yourself, Ray. I know some real world-class ingrates. You're not one of them. How did you meet Oliver, anyway?"

"Some studio executive brought him on a tour when we were shooting *Double Indemnity*. He heard that I was doing the screenplay, so he came to my office and introduced himself."

Martha shook her head and looked down at her desk. "I didn't even know he'd been to California." I didn't say anything. She said, "You could give me one of those cigarettes that you're fiddling with."

We lit up, and I still didn't know what to say. She said, "My nerves aren't terribly steady, either. Running this hotel is like having a persistent headache." She looked up and smiled at me. "If I were doing my job, I'd ask you if your room is satisfactory."

"Of course it is, Martha, for God's sake. Do you have to run this place all by yourself?"

"Not entirely, no. I've actually found a very good manager."

"What's his name?"

"Walter Vertsag. He's German."

"How old is he?"

"Why on earth would you want to know that?"

I took a long pull on my cigarette. "I've heard his name before."

She stepped back into herself a little. "He must be about sixty. Although he seems younger. He's very fit. I still want to know why you're asking."

"I'm just being nosy. But what I really don't understand is why you're here while Oliver is living over in the States."

"Raymond – if I explain that, will you explain why you're here while your wife is in California?"

"*Touché*. I guess I'm not fit company for decent people these days."

I got up to leave, but she said, "I'm not offended, Ray. I've been fairly shirty myself." She stood up and held out her hand. "No hard feelings?"

"Absolutely none. And I'm sorry to have stuck my nose into your business."

"No offence taken. All I know, Raymond, is that business in this hotel has blossomed since I hired Walter. I really wouldn't care if he was Hitler's cook. I was worried sick that if Oliver stopped sending money, I'd be facing old age without a penny. Now I can take care of myself nicely, thank you. Without Oliver or anybody else."

After supper I grabbed a newspaper from the lobby. I knew I couldn't just throw myself into bed and go to sleep. I never could. I seemed to live in some in-between state, yawning through the day and then lying wide-eyed in bed at night.

I glanced at the headlines while I walked back to my room. The lead story was about Israel. They had declared themselves to be a nation a few weeks earlier. The British had been in charge of that part of the world since World War One – they called it a

"Protectorate" – but they'd seen the handwriting on the wall and pulled out. Now the Arab armies were fighting to push the Israelis out. It was a hell of a mess, and I couldn't imagine how it would ever be resolved. My sympathies were with the Jews, but the Palestinians were getting a raw deal too.

A few years back I'd talked with Billy Wilder about Palestine. Millions of Jews wanted to move there, but the British government had set up an immigration quota. Wilder had supported an organization that smuggled them in. They'd concocted new names and new identity papers, and they'd organized midnight landings onto Palestinian beaches. I wondered if the people-smuggling was still going on. With Israel on its own two feet, they probably didn't need to.

I didn't like Wilder personally. When we worked together on the *Double Indemnity* screenplay, he was always jabbing a pencil at me and interrupting every time I opened my mouth. I never got to finish a sentence when he was in the room, but in spite of everything I admired the little bastard. His parents had died in concentration camps, and he wasn't going to let anybody push him around. He knew the price you'd pay if you did.

Like everybody else, I'd seen the photos from the camps. Skeletal people, starving, terrified – while the rest of us had hunkered down in our burrows, collecting our paychecks and ignoring the rumors. A few of the bastards who'd built those hellholes were being put on trial, but thousands of them were slipping away to South America. A few people had the guts to track them down. Me, I wrote detective stories.

I pulled my letter to Cissy out of my shirt pocket. What was I doing over here, anyway? Trying to recapture my lost youth? My youth had been a miserable grind, and I'd never been happier than the day I sailed to America. Until the day I met Cissy Pascal.

Warren and Alma Lloyd held soirées on Friday evenings, and they invited me to join them. Their roomy house on South Bonnie Brae drew a witty crowd of well-educated and well-heeled Angelinos who sang and danced and listened with attention when Alma recited her poetry. Even as tongue-tied as I was, I found myself discussing *Isis Unveiled* and fooling around over a Ouija board with a roomful of well-mannered strangers. Estelle would serve canapés and touch my shoulder lightly while I struggled to learn Russian Whist. And every Friday Warren would challenge me to a chess game and beat me to a pulp.

It was on one of those evenings that I looked up from the chessboard and saw a gorgeous woman dancing. She was dancing alone, swaying with a sleepy energy and tilting her head back to accent her lovely long neck and throat. At the piano, a starchy old buzzard in a black suit was playing a haunting melody I'd never heard before.

I'd just beaten Warren at chess for the first time. I'd lured him into a trap with a Queen sacrifice, and I was buzzing with adrenaline. I stood up and bowed to the dancing woman – just a notch. She looked at me with luminous, teasing eyes, and I started dancing with her. Separately but in perfect harmony, we swayed and spun in an improvised arm's-length waltz. We challenged each other with our glances. *Can you follow this? You bet I can. Can you do this? Just watch me.*

It was only when the music reached its elegant, inevitable conclusion that we touched fingers. After that, I never looked back.

I checked my watch. Midnight in Ireland, four in the afternoon in California. I could try to call her, but I hesitated to try. I was too weary, and too likely to put my foot in my mouth. Enough was enough. I got up to draw the curtains when I saw the two men in the parking lot. They were lifting suitcases out of the hotel bus and into the back of a delivery van. The shorter guy walked with a rolling gait, like somebody who'd had rickets. The taller one was Bocklett.

I thought about going down to see what they were doing, but I didn't. I had a clammy feeling in my guts, an ugly worry that I'd be biting off more than I could chew. I slipped off my shoes and lay down on the quilt that covered the bed. As I fell asleep I heard the deep throb of a ship's whistle, like the lowest note on a pipe organ, far out at sea.

Chapter Four

In the Renvyle House dining room, the morning sun streamed through cut-glass windows that refracted rainbows onto the walls. The waiter rolled a cart with a heavy silver tea-service to my table. I said, "Do you have coffee?"

"Yes, Sir. It will take a few minutes to prepare. May I bring you some cornflakes?"

"God, no. I want a big Irish breakfast."

He lifted an eyebrow. "Many of our customers ask for a bowl of cornflakes to begin their breakfast."

"They can have it. Cornflakes are a cockeyed American idea, anyway. Baby food."

He walked away, leaving a whiff of disdain in the air. I wished that I'd asked for a cup of tea while the coffee was brewing. It had taken years to wean myself from tea to coffee when I moved from England to America. Now I couldn't get enough of the stuff.

I leafed through a fresh newspaper. It was full of cryptic headlines like ASSIZES OPTION REMANDED TO BYE-ELECTION, followed by turgid descriptions of governmental paper-shuffling. Most of the other articles were about farming or sports, a mix of rugby, hurling, and something called Gaelic Football. There were a few international stories buried on page six. The Nuremberg trials were still going on, now with a bunch of German industrial executives in the dock. That made sense. They were the ones who'd bankrolled the Nazis in the first place.

I knew who he was as soon as he stepped into the dining room. Sleek black hair, combed to perfection. An expensive double-breasted black suit, white shirt, dark tie. I couldn't see his shoes, but I knew they'd gleam. The kind of senior officer who'd chew the lieutenants' asses unmercifully, who'd be pissed off if he couldn't find something to criticize. Cold as a steel knife. He consulted with the headwaiter, glanced in my direction, and walked across the room to my table. We eyed each other for a few seconds. He said, "It's Mister Thornton, isn't it?"

It wasn't a question. I said, "You must be the manager."

He nodded about a sixteenth of an inch. He had eyes like a snake. "Walter Vertsag. I trust that you are enjoying your stay in the hotel."

That wasn't a question either. I wondered what would happen if I asked him to hurry up the coffee, but he beat me to the punch. "I understand that you are a personal friend of Mrs Gogarty. We appreciate your efforts in helping Mrs Yeats find her cat."

"Glad to do it. How's the puss, anyway?"

"I understand that it is still alive. May I ask who helped you yesterday?"

"Who helped me?"

"The man who was with you in the seaweed baths."

We stared at each other for a while. I said, "A guy I met in a pub."

"A local man?"

"Can't tell you. I didn't get to know him."

He took a few seconds to choose his weapon before he spoke. "I don't think that I need to remind you, Sir, that we maintain a certain standard in this hotel."

I felt like a specimen under a microscope. I said, "Groucho Marx."

"I beg your pardon?"

"Groucho Marx said he'd never join a club that would accept a person like him as a member."

"I understand you are a writer, Sir, and writers can be very witty. But sometimes writers stray into areas that are…"

"That are what?"

"Sensitive."

"What the hell is that supposed to mean?"

A voice said, "Excuse me, Sir," and the waiter reached over my shoulder with the breakfast-plate. The food smelled delicious, and my stomach growled. Vertsag smirked a little. He'd gotten under my skin, and he knew it. "I meant no offence, Mister Chandler. Please contact me if I can help you in any way."

"Your coffee, Sir?" I twisted around to say *Yeah, thanks,* and when I turned back, Vertsag had disappeared like a magician in a vanishing act. I tore into the bacon and sausages and eggs, and I burned with resentment. I'd let him call me by my name.

I kicked myself while I drove to Wittgenstein's cottage. What would Marlowe have done? He'd have told Vertsag where to stick his breakfast – no, he wouldn't lower himself to that. But he'd have walked away, out of the dining room, without a backward glance. Out of the hotel? Absolutely.

And he'd have had the last word. *Writers tell the truth. And they don't owe anybody a damned thing.* Something like that. Or something stronger.

Marlowe, Marlowe. He was more real to me than most people were. And I suspected that when people said they wanted to meet me, they really wanted to meet him. Why would they want to meet a nervous guy who wolfs his breakfast without tasting it, or who drives his car too fast when he's mad at himself? They'd do better to meet Bogie, or Dick Powell.

I hit the brakes to slow down for a sharp left turn. I'd been tearing along between two stone walls that were about eight feet apart, startling sheep that grazed in the weeds along the verge. I'd have a miserable time apologizing to Martha Gogarty if I splattered her Rolls with sheep's blood.

The road to Wittgenstein's cottage ended with a gravelled turnaround in front of an old stone barn and some abandoned outbuildings. I parked the car and walked down the footpath to the cottage. I stopped to catch my breath at the edge of the concrete dock. I was badly out of shape. Carney's boat rocked and strained at the hawsers in the low swells of Killary Harbor. The tires that hung over the sides of the boat scraped against the side of the concrete dock. The water glistened with a dark rainbow of oil and gasoline. *Petrol*, I reminded myself – it's *petrol* over here. *Petrol* made more sense, since it came from *petroleum*, but it still sounded pompous. Like *tyres*.

I knocked at the cottage door. There was some scraping and banging, and the latch clacked open. He staggered a little at the door, like a prisoner coming out of solitary confinement. I said, "Ludwig, I need to tell you – I've heard some things..."

"I am writing, Raymond. I need to finish what I am doing."

We looked at each other for a few seconds. He shifted his weight like a man with stiff legs, but he didn't blink. I said, "Okay. I'll come back."

"Get something for yourself if you want." He turned back into the cottage and left the door open. He bent over the table, and I could hear his pen scratching. I walked in, found a tea-stained mug in the sink and filled it with water. He kept on writing. I stepped outside, shut the door and lit a cigarette.

I didn't take offense at Wittgenstein. I had a reputation for being a prickly writer, too. It was one of those choices you had to make. You had to set aside the private hours each day to work, and you had to lock the door. It didn't matter if your Aunt Prunella died, or if she left you a million in her will, or both. Writing time was sacrosanct, and if anybody tried to interrupt, you had to tell them to piss off.

But I wasn't writing. I hadn't written anything worth a damn for six years. Wilder and I had been nominated for an Oscar for the screenplay for *Double Indemnity*, but it was Jim Cain's story and Wilder's movie and I could barely stand to look at myself in the mirror after it was released. In Hollywood they called it *collaborating*. HUAC had a different definition of *collaborating*.

And I couldn't get the Nuremberg trials out of my head. They had prosecuted a few unspeakable bastards who deserved to be locked up or hanged, but I wondered if the whole business wasn't a show-trial, a distraction to keep us preoccupied while the others slipped away. I wondered how they managed their getaways – the passports, the tickets, the aliases – but I knew what Marlowe would say about that. *If you've got the cash, there isn't anyplace you can't go.* And they had plenty of cash. They'd looted Europe for years.

I sat on an old crate and looked across the bay. The vegetation on the hills grew in layers of green upon green, accented with splotches of purple heather and bright yellow gorse. They called the gorse *furze*, a word I liked. I wondered if *furze* could be transplanted from Connemara to California. It would probably shrivel to dust in a week. And I could imagine what Cissy would say if I showed up with a suitcase full of plants. *Does this mean that we're rich again, Raymio? Are we getting a gardener, too?*

In 1914 we never argued or worried about money. We danced. At those Friday evening soirées, Cissy would follow me in an easy two-step for a few bars before she'd pull free and improvize, graceful as a cat. Then she'd slide back into my arms, and we'd twirl like butterflies in a moonbeam. Other dancers would move aside to watch us, and I wished that the music would never stop.

We did some of our best dancing when her husband played the piano. Cissy would glide in graceful arabesques while Julian shifted the tempo and I tried to keep a lid on the yearning that bubbled up in my heart. When the others applauded, I wondered how much of our three-way tug-of-war they could see.

When Cissy mingled and charmed her way around the room, I'd sit and drink with Julian. I did most of the talking while he felt his pulse or dabbed at his forehead with a handkerchief. When he talked, he talked to the floor. From the scraps of information I could pull out of him, I gathered that he was old enough to be my father. His son Gordon was nearly my age, and I worried about what that might mean until Julian told me that he'd been married to Gordon's mother before he met Cissy. Gordon had inherited Julian's beak of a nose, but he looked twice as healthy as his skinny, fidgeting father. I made myself miserable by speculating about Cissy and Julian making love.

Cissy never bothered to speculate about anything. She was always *there*, dancing and talking and touching. It was the touching that did it for me. When we talked, she'd graze the back of my hand with her fingertips. She seldom touched Julian. Sometimes she'd put her hand on his shoulder when she leaned over to look at the sheet music on the keyboard, but otherwise she kept her distance from him. I wondered if he was queer.

Julian and Cissy rarely missed a Friday-night soirée, and Warren and Alma brought them along on their automotive jaunts up and down the Pacific coast. I tried to un-pick the social calculus that went on in the Lloyd household. Did Alma invite Julian because he was a composer? Did Julian share Warren's infatuation with Madame Blavatsky and all of that Theosophical foofaraw? Or did Warren invite Julian because he liked to watch Cissy dance?

I threw my cigarette into the water. It hissed and floated for a minute before it started to disintegrate. I wanted to phone my wife. I wanted to tell her about Wittgenstein, and about Vertsag, and about Georgie's cat. And about what Bocklett had said to me. I wanted to tell her that I wasn't just suffering from a persecution complex after all.

I stood up, stretched, and walked along the dock toward Carney's boat. The tide was out, and the boat rode in the low water six feet down from the edge of the concrete. Someone had left the hatch open, and I could see a tangle of pipes and hoses in a murky compartment below the deck. I had a flicker of a good-samaritan impulse to jump down and close the hatch, but I decided against it.

I thought about the shadowy pantomime I'd seen in the hotel parking lot, and I wondered what they were up to. I kicked myself for my gutless worries. Nothing bad seemed likely in the Connemara sunshine. But Marlowe wouldn't have hesitated to put his nickel in, and if I had another chance, I wouldn't hesitate either.

Wittgenstein emerged from the gloom of the cottage. He held up a handful of breadcrumbs, and two robins fluttered down from the eaves to eat out of his hand. I watched his saintly pantomime until he noticed me. "Raymond! How long have you been out here?"

"A while. I don't know."

"I am glad to see you. I have been writing something that I want to ask you about."

"What's that?"

"Aspect-seeing."

"Okay, Ludwig, whatever that is. But I've got something to tell you, too." We went into the cottage. I said, "Would you mind if I make some coffee?"

"There is no coffee, Raymond – you can make tea if you like." He scribbled something on a page. I filled the kettle and put it on the gas-ring. It groaned and rumbled as the water started to heat up. I sat down across the table from him. He was writing in the margins of a notebook that was already full. He looked like he could do that all day.

"Ludwig," I said, "There's something I need to tell you. I hope I'm wrong, but I think we both need to be careful."

"What are you talking about, Raymond?"

"The hotel manager asked me about you this morning. I didn't tell him anything, but I imagine it won't take him long to figure out who you are, and where you live."

"Why does that worry you? I am curious about him as well."

"Maybe it's just my imagination, but after what you told me about that Lieutenant Vertsag..."

Wittgenstein shook his head. "It would be no great loss if someone shot me, Raymond."

"Are you serious?"

"Absolutely. Death has been my companion for as long as I can remember."

I stared at the grimy window of the cottage and said, "I get worried when people talk like that."

"You should not worry about me, Raymond. I believe that the war sorted us out. You and I were both chosen to live."

We saved a lot of you Army guys from getting shot. I thought that surviving a war had more to do with dumb luck than with fate, and I tried to think of a diplomatic way to say that until I realized that he was scribbling again.

I said, "Are you writing or editing?"

"I am writing only for myself."

"A first draft, or…"

"I jump all around the topic. That is the only way of thinking that is natural to me. Forcing my thoughts into an ordered sequence is a torment."

"You're not the only writer who has that problem."

"Only every so often does one of the sentences I am writing here make a step forward. The rest are like the snipping of the barber's scissors, which he has to keep in motion so as to be able to make a cut with them at the right moment."

"But what are you writing *about*?"

He put down his pen. "Do you remember what I said about aspects?"

"More or less. Isn't an aspect something like a point of view?"

"That's partially correct."

"Can you give me an example?"

He flipped back through the notebook. "Here – two people are laughing together, at a joke perhaps. One of them has said certain somewhat unusual words and now they both break out into a sort of bleating."

"I'm with you so far."

"I've written that this might appear very bizarre to someone arriving among us from a quite different background. Whereas we find it quite reasonable."

"I always thought that people laughed at things that weren't reasonable…"

"No, I mean the act of laughing itself." He glared again. I didn't know what to say. He said, "I witnessed this scene recently on a bus. I was able to think myself into the skin of someone not accustomed to it. It struck me then as quite irrational, and like the reactions of an outlandish animal."

"I don't think I can buy that one, Ludwig. I think that humor is one of the things that makes us human."

"It is cultural, Raymond."

I said, "I think some things are beyond culture. Like silent movies. And cartoons."

"Cartoons?"

"Yeah, that's a better example. Take your optical illusion, for instance. Do you have a sheet of paper?" Wittgenstein handed me one of his notebooks and opened it to a blank page. I drew two drabbits, with a circle for the eye in one, and an x in the other. I said, "Okay – what do you see?"

"It is as I said before, Raymond. It depends on the aspect from which we see it. It is both a rabbit and a duck..."

"The eyes, Ludwig. What do they tell you?"

"The eyes?" He pointed to the one with the x for its eye. "This one is dead."

I felt as proud as if I'd done a back-flip and landed on my feet. "And I'll bet that if we showed this to a Hindu or a Chinaman, they'd say the same thing."

Wittgenstein stared at the paper a while longer. "It might be blind. Or asleep."

"You're thinking about it too much. And you're stepping on my punch line." We sat there for a while. Finally I said, "Talk about culture – the whole world just finished a long, ugly war with a culture that forgot how to laugh at itself."

Wittgenstein shook his head. "Humour is not a mood. It is a way of looking at the world. So, if it is right to say that humour was eradicated in Nazi Germany, that does not mean that people were not in good spirits or anything of the sort, but something much deeper and more important."

"I think that's what I'm trying to say. If anybody had ever taught that guy how to laugh, or not to take himself so seriously – maybe when he was about fourteen..."

"I knew him then, Raymond."

"Are you kidding? *Der Führer?*"

"We were students together at the *Realschule* in Linz. We were born only a few days apart."

"Christ Almighty. What was he like?"

"I cannot say. He spoke to no one. Of course, neither did I. Excuse me for one moment."

Wittgenstein turned back to his notebook. The kettle on the ring stopped groaning and sent up a plume of steam. While I made two cups of tea, I wondered if I could get him to say more about his old schoolmate. The personality of that dark, remorseless man still hovered over the world like a cloud of smoke after a bombing. Most of the men I knew – the Gentiles, anyway – would confess, usually after a few drinks, that they were fascinated by Adolf Hitler. They'd shake their heads in half-admiration – *He went too far, but he really had something, you know...*

And what the hell had happened to him? The official story was that he'd committed suicide in his bunker, but nobody could find his body. Maybe the Russians had him. Or maybe he'd shaved off that moustache and slipped away to Argentina.

I'd thought about Nazis when my ship to Ireland had docked in Panama City. The locals had brought out their souvenir stands, and I walked down the gangplank to buy a straw hat. I didn't try to sneak past the Panamanian immigration officers, but they didn't look like they'd pose much of a challenge. Anybody with money in his pocket and some kind of passport could catch a train from there to Buenos Aires or Asunción. I'd thought about writing a story about Nazis in South America, but it didn't seem like Marlowe's line of work. It didn't seem to be anybody's.

My stomach rumbled. I said, "Do you have anything to eat around here?"

He slid a cardboard box across the table. "Perhaps you would like one of these?"

The label said *Charcoal Biscuits*. I nibbled at one of the little grey cookies and said, "I can see why Tommy's wife worries about your diet. Do you like these things?"

"They are a relief for *die Magenschmerzen.*"

"I imagine they'll either cure you or kill you." Wittgenstein shrugged. I said, "If your stomach is really upset, you ought to get some milk of magnesia. Or take one of those seaweed baths. They're supposed to be good for settling your nerves."

"Have you taken one, Raymond?"

"No, I haven't."

He looked at me for a moment. "No one can think a thought for me. In the same way, no one can don my hat for me."

"Sorry, Ludwig. I'm a fine one to be giving advice. My stomach usually feels like a knot in a wet sheet."

He smiled. "That is well-said, Raymond. A good simile refreshes the intellect. But what is ragged should be left ragged."

I sipped at the tea and thought that one over. I couldn't figure out whether I'd been complimented or chastised. I wondered if other people felt like they were failing an intelligence test when they tried to talk with him.

The engine of Carney's boat roared into life. I said, "Hang on a minute, Ludwig," and I hurried out onto the dock. Carney had loosened the mooring ropes, and he jumped down to the rear deck of the boat. I ran across the concrete and yelled *Hey!* He looked up at me with a blank stare. I said, "What would it cost to go fishing?"

He pointed at his ear, shook his head, and pretended to be busy coiling the hawsers. The engine was loud, but I knew he could hear me. I leaned down and and yelled, "I want to go fishing!"

"Can't help you." He stashed the rope and turned toward the cabin.

I said, "What about Bocklett?"

He stopped and looked at me. "Who's askin'?"

"I want to go out. With you and Bocklett."

He looked at my city clothes. "You with the Yanks?"

"No, I just sound like a Yank. I'm a Brit."

"Then get your own fuckin' boat." He stepped into the cabin, slammed the door and spun the wheel. The engine roared louder, and the boat pulled away from the dock.

"Raymond?"

I had no idea how long Wittgenstein had been standing beside me. He said, "What are you doing out here?"

We watched Carney's boat move across the harbor and toward the sea. I said, "I can write 'em, but I can't make 'em happen."

"What are you talking about, Raymond?" Wittgenstein stared at me the way that you'd stare at a demented bum who was talking to himself on a street-corner.

"I told him too much. And I didn't learn a goddamn thing."

"What were you hoping to learn?"

I felt like a kid who's been caught playing with matches. I said, "I was just fishing."

Wittgenstein looked at me again with those unblinking eyes. "Will you explain this to me, Raymond?"

"I'm not sure I can. Let's go back inside."

Wittgenstein watched while I tried to drink my tea. My hands shook. I hated making an ass of myself. Why had I said anything to Carney about Bocklett? I could have created a nasty mess for myself. And maybe for Wittgenstein. I fought an impulse to leave and go stick my head in the sand. I said, "Ludwig, I need some advice. Some philosophical advice."

"I think you may be disappointed, Raymond. That is not the purpose of philosophy."

"Okay. Forget philosophy. I just need a friend." He looked worried, but I went on. "First of all, you're right – I'm the guy who wrote that book in the car. And a couple of others."

He smiled. "Then perhaps I am a good detective?"

"You're probably a better one than I am. I'm not Philip Marlowe."

He nodded. "But why do you travel *inkognito*?"

"That's what I want to talk with you about. Have you ever heard of the House Un-American Activities Committee?"

"I cannot make sense of that name."

"You're not alone. It's a bunch of congressmen from the House of Representatives. They're getting their names into the newspapers by looking for communists."

"That should not be difficult. There are plenty of communists in Russia."

"That's not where they're looking. They think that there's some kind of communist fifth column in America that's trying to upset the applecart. Take over the government, nationalize General Motors – you know?" Wittgenstein looked blank. I could see that he'd never read a newspaper in his life. I said, "There are a lot of people who are scared to death of communism because they've been told that it's like slavery. Or that the Reds are going to steal their money. Most of them don't know the first thing about it, but they've been convinced that it's a great evil plot to destroy America. And a lot of people are getting rich by keeping those fears whipped up."

Wittgenstein took a deep breath. "I went to Russia a few years ago, Raymond. I wanted to work there in a factory. But they offered me only teaching jobs."

"Didn't you want to work as a teacher?"

"But that was not my intention. I had heard that the Russian people embraced communism with a religious fervour. I wanted to discover what that was like."

"So were they fervent?"

"Not at all. Most people had to be dishonest to survive. Life there is very sad and difficult, like being a private in the Army. And they're frightened of America."

"The Congressmen I'm talking about would say that you've been brainwashed. They'd say that everything that you tell them about Russia would be a lie."

"Then how could we possibly discuss…"

"You couldn't. The chairman of HUAC is a son of a bitch named Parnell Thomas, and he isn't interested in discussing anything. None of them are. They made a big stink about investigating the State Department, and it got their names in the newspaper. That's the kind of publicity that helps get them re-elected. Now they're going after Hollywood." Wittgenstein shook his head. I said, "They put ten guys in jail for Contempt of

Congress. Mostly screenwriters, and a couple of directors. And now they're publishing lists of everybody they suspect. If your name's on that list, you're screwed. Nobody in Hollywood will hire you, and no publisher will touch you. It's character assassination, with teeth."

"Have they investigated you, Raymond?"

"No, but they're thinking about it."

"How do you know that?"

"My agent warned me that it was a possibility. And then somebody else confirmed it. Just yesterday."

Wittgenstein still looked puzzled. "But you are very American, Raymond. When anyone thinks of America, they think of detectives. Or cowboys. Why would they investigate you?"

"Have you ever read that book? The one in the back seat of the car?"

"I don't think so."

"In that one, Marlowe meets a security guard on a private road. They start talking, and they agree that they can't stand the rich phonies who live on private roads with security guards."

"That sounds like something that Philip Marlowe would say."

"Then the security guard says that he knows a guy who belongs to a John Reed Club, over in Boyle Heights. And Marlowe says *Tovarich*."

"And what is a John Reed Club?"

"It used to be a bunch of lefties who got together in the evenings. They fell apart after Stalin signed that non-aggression pact with your old schoolmate." We looked at each other. I said, "So do you understand why I worry about being investigated?"

"Not at all."

"My book is just exactly what those simple-minded bastards are looking for. They'll say *Chandler's a communist. He calls everybody Comrade.*"

"But if it isn't true..."

"It doesn't have to be true. My publisher would drop me like a hot potato. And the American Legion would throw my books out of every library in the country."

"Would the libraries not need to replace them, then?"

"Oh, Christ, Ludwig – you should be my agent. You're the only guy in the world who'd see a Congressional investigation as a sales opportunity."

I walked to the door. Carney and his boat were gone. The sun was shining on Killary Harbor, and a seagull was pecking at something in a tangle of ropes. I said, "I probably shouldn't have mentioned any of this..."

"I am the one who should be sorry, Raymond. I'm afraid that I have disappointed you."

"No, it's not like that. I don't exactly know what I'm asking you for." The seagull flapped away with something in its beak. I said, "I may be pushed into a situation that I can't avoid. Has anyone ever asked you for advice when they were being threatened?"

"Yes, one of my students came to me when he was conscripted."

"And what did you tell him?"

"I told him that if he ever got mixed up in hand-to-hand fighting, he should just stand aside and let himself be massacred."

I turned around and stared at Wittgenstein. He looked perfectly serious. "Ludwig," I said, "that's not what I was hoping to hear."

"What do you want me to say, Raymond? Should I tell you to lie to them? Or to hide?"

"What do you think I'm doing over here?"

Wittgenstein stood up from the table. In the shadowy room he looked exactly like the severe schoolmaster who would cuff the boys' ears and pull the girls' hair. "There is no escape, Raymond.

And there is no compromise. You cannot be reluctant to give up your lie and still tell the truth."

"Whose idea is that? Rebecca of Sunnybrook Farm?"

"If the truth is not strong enough to sustain us, then life is hopeless."

I said, "Detectives never tell the truth if they can help it."

He looked genuinely shocked. "You cannot mean that, Raymond. If they are not searching for the truth…"

"That's a quote from your friend Norbert Davis. I think it's from *Rendezvous with Fear*."

"Then it is a quote from Doan and not from Norbert Davis. Were you not telling me that people confuse you with Philip Marlowe?"

I shook my head. "Ludwig, I give up. If I get a subpoena, those guys will eat me for lunch, no matter whaFt I say. And when they're finished with me, they'll probably go after Bert Davis."

Wittgenstein looked out the window and said, "Your country frightens me."

"It frightens me, too."

We sat there for a while, listening to the waves lapping at the dock. Wittgenstein said, "Do you think that Norbert Davis is in danger?"

"I know he's going through a rough spell. None of his stories have been optioned by the studios since before the war."

"What does that mean, Raymond?"

"Nobody is making his books into movies. That's the only way to make any serious money in this business. You might be able to take a vacation on your publishing royalties, but most writers can't afford to live on their book sales. You must know that, Ludwig. You've written books, haven't you?"

"Only the *Tractatus*."

"Did you receive any royalties?"

"I have no idea."

"God Almighty. Anyway, I got a letter from Bert Davis last year. He's broke. I loaned him two hundred dollars."

"Are you asking me to send money to him?"

"If you feel like sending him money, I'm sure he can use it. But I think that a letter from you would mean a lot to him."

"I must confess that I have thought about writing to him, Raymond. But I do not want to obligate him to write back to me."

"I don't think he'd take it that way..."

"I am never certain about these things. I wrote to Bertrand Russell because he was a philosopher. But I do not know how it is with other people."

"It's just like a conversation. You can end it whenever you want to."

"But in a conversation, one person throws a ball. The other does not know – is he to throw it back, throw it to a third person, or leave it lying, or pick it up and put it in his pocket?"

"Ludwig, I think you may be the only person I know who's more neurotic than me."

"What are you saying, Raymond?" He looked hurt.

"All I know is this. When I was scratching to make a living from my stories, any letter was a huge lift. It's what we write for, isn't it? The recognition?"

"That is not why I write."

"Well, I can guarantee you that Norbert Davis writes for recognition. And so does Dashiell Hammett and Cornell Woolrich and everybody else I know. And Bert Davis is in a hell of a slump. A letter from you would lift his spirits a mile."

Wittgenstein shook his head. "I receive letters from many people, but most of them have no understanding of my work. If I would try to answer all of them..."

"Maybe that's one of the differences between novelists and philosophers. If Schrödinger wrote to you, wouldn't you be pleased?"

"He is not a philosopher, but yes, I would be pleased. Do people write to you, Raymond?"

"Oh, yes. Mostly they want me to read their manuscripts, or recommend them to my agent, or get them a movie contract. I don't bother with those. But a few people just write to say that they genuinely enjoyed reading something I wrote. That's what makes it worthwhile."

"Do you write to other writers to encourage them?"

"Not nearly enough. But you've reminded me of something. You were talking about America, and detectives and cowboys..."

"Yes."

"I got a letter once from W. H. Auden. Or my publisher did, and that amounts to the same thing. He said that I'd brought the 'Man of the West' into the big dirty city, or words to that effect. It made me feel great."

"And did you answer his letter?"

"Actually, I didn't. I was still thinking about it when he wrote an article for *Harper's* about detective stories. In there he said that my books were 'depressing.' What the hell am I supposed to say to that?"

"I know that article, Raymond. He also said that your books should be read as serious literature."

"I wish they generated more serious income. Anyway, it was nice to get a mash note from the old poof."

Wittgenstein looked like I'd kicked him in the stomach. "I don't think you should say things like that, Raymond."

"Oh, I'm just talking to hear myself talk..."

"No, Raymond. I think you should go now."

"Ludwig, I'm sorry. I didn't mean anything..."

He shook his head and walked out of the cottage. I sat there feeling like a kid who's had his knuckles rapped, and I knew I deserved it. By the time I got up and stepped to the door, Wittgenstein was already thirty yards up the path. I stood there, wanting to call him back and wishing I'd kept my mouth shut. I fumbled for a cigarette, and after I got it lit I couldn't see him any more. For a skinny guy who didn't know how to feed himself, he had an angry energy that I'd never be able to overtake. Marlowe could have caught up with him, but Marlowe would never have shot off his mouth in the first place.

I walked back to the car and drove slowly along the road toward Renvyle. I couldn't see a trace of Wittgenstein. Footpaths led off the road in all directions. I hoped he'd headed inland, and not out toward the sea-cliffs.

Chapter Five

In the Renvyle House parking lot I sat in the Rolls for a long time, worrying about Wittgenstein. I wondered how many more relationships I could screw up in my life. I seemed to have a talent for it.

When the war broke out in 1914, I brought my mother over from England to Los Angeles. She moved into my apartment and cooked my meals while I balanced the books at the creamery. I hesitated to let her know about the Lloyds' Friday-night soirées, but when Warren and Alma asked me to bring her along, she put on her best clothes and fussed with her hair and looked ten years younger by the time we got there. She chatted with Alma and took her turn at the Ouija boards with an enthusiasm that surprised me. I introduced her to Cissy and Julian, wondering what they'd think of her. Julian asked her gracious questions about her life in England, and she mumbled shy answers.

Later my mother pulled me aside. "How old is that woman, Raymond?"

"Oh, in her thirties, I suppose."

"And how old is her husband?"

"I have no idea. They look like a May-December match."

My mother arched an eyebrow. "I think September is more like it."

We let it drop. I thought she was talking about Julian.

After my mother moved in, my apartment felt like a prison. Except for our Friday evenings with the Lloyds, she never went out, and she barely spoke ten words a day. I'd made good on my promise to my uncle, but I felt trapped like an insect in amber, or one of those eyeless fish who live too deep in the ocean for the light to penetrate.

Except when I was near Cissy. The Lloyds began including my mother and me along with Cissy and Julian on their automotive ventures up and down the Pacific Coast Highway. On the face of it, we must have looked like a gang of rich *Angelinos* who were having the time of our lives. We drank wine with our picnic lunches and abalone steak dinners, and we chuckled over the hand-painted souvenirs in the roadside markets. Julian sat with Warren and Alma on the wide front seat – he claimed that he got carsick unless he sat in front – while I wedged myself between my mother and Cissy in the back. Her every touch, bump and jostle felt like a wordless conversation. Cissy treated me to an occasional sideways glance that sent my heart spinning. I couldn't spend five seconds without thinking about her.

In October Warren drove all of us to San Francisco, motoring up Highway One for two endless days. After we checked into our hotel rooms, Julian asked me to come down to the bar for a drink. When he told the bartender to put it on his room tab, I started to make the usual protest about splitting the bill, but Julian surprised me by grabbing my arm. He said, "I'm paying for this. I don't want to owe you a thing."

"But I'm planning to drink as much as you do."

"Forget that. I'm not blind, you know."

Instead of talking to the floor, he was staring at me. I heard myself saying, "Nobody ever said you were blind..."

"Don't patronize me."

"I don't know what you're talking about."

"Bullshit. You've been like a dog on the hunt. Leave Cissy alone."

My heart was pounding, and my voice felt strangled. "What do you mean?"

"I'll tell you what I mean. Do you know what *Alienation of Affection* means?"

"I've heard of it..."

"It means I can sue you. Right now, if I want to. It means lawyers, and lawyers cost money, and I have a lot more money than you do. I can ruin you."

I couldn't meet his eyes. I said, "You're making a mistake..."

"You're the one who's making a mistake. If I were younger, I'd take you out in the back alley and settle this personally. But I won't hesitate to have a lawyer do it for me."

"For Christ's sake, Julian. What do you want?"

"Don't try to throw this back at me, you little shit. You're the one who sweet-talks my wife and then hides behind your mother's skirts..."

"Leave my mother out of this!"

We glared at each other for a while. Finally he said, "Do you have any guts? Real guts?"

"What the hell are you talking about?"

"There's a war going on, if you haven't noticed. Gordon's joining the Canadian Army. He wants to find out what kind of man he is." He looked me up and down. "What kind of man are you?"

I didn't know what to say. He stood up and put a dollar tip on the bar. "I'm going back upstairs. To sleep with my wife. I don't give a fuck what you do. Just keep your hands off her."

I took the night train back to Los Angeles. I phoned the Canadian Consulate, made sure that they'd pay my mother an allowance, and told them that I was an English citizen who wanted to join their Army. They told me to report for induction in Vancouver. I felt like I was emerging from a three-year fug.

Cissy's letter reached me after a week of basic training.

Ray, for the love of God, have you lost your mind? It's like a slaughterhouse over there. Julian bullied Gordon into going, and now you. I'll never forgive him. There aren't many chances for magic in life, and we have one of those chances. If you don't get killed or crippled, of course. Is that the way you want it?

She rambled on for a few more paragraphs urging me to protect myself and not take risks. *I want you back all in one piece. All I can do until then is hunker down and hope. You mean too much to me. Please write and write and write to me. If I can't have you here, at least I can have your letters.*

With all my love,
Cissy

PS – Your mother is going to live with us while you're away.

Northern France was as green as Ireland, except for the sea of mud along the trenches. By the time I got there, both sides were overstretched and exhausted. They made me a sergeant, and my main job was to convince my squad not to bunch up when we were ordered to attack. *The machine-gunners are going to look for clusters of us to shoot at. For Christ's sake spread out.* We went over the top, pissing down our legs, and half of us didn't come back.

I didn't take a bullet, but I got a bad concussion in a mortar attack. They sent me back to England and started teaching me how to fly a fighter plane when the word came down that the whole thing was over. They'd signed an Armistice. Ten million soldiers and seven million civilians dead for a goddamned piece of paper.

On the troop transports back to Vancouver, a few yokels tried to drum up enthusiasm for beer parties and victorious hoopla, but most of us were sick of it – sick of taking orders, sick of seeing death, sick of the ugly choices that we'd made to stay alive. And on the long train ride from Seattle to Los Angeles, reading over the letters that Cissy had sent me week after week, I wondered what sort of tangle I was going to find when I got there.

After two acrimonious weeks, Estelle Lloyd suggested that we ask her father for help. He had a knack for managing human behavior. He'd even written a book called *Psychology Normal and Abnormal*. I wondered which category he'd put us in.

Warren told us to carry the kitchen chairs into the living room, and I thought it was a good idea. Cissy and Julian had a two-seater couch, but who was going to sit on it? It was their house, and they were the logical ones to perch there, but with their marriage coming unglued, it didn't seem like a good idea. Cissy and I could have sat there, since we were the ones who were causing the problem, but I didn't have the nerve to suggest it. It struck me that Julian could sit on the couch with my mother. They were the only ones in the room who weren't romantically involved, but part of me wished that they were. Julian was older than my mother, and he could have made a good husband for her. Better than my father had, anyway. Maurice Chandler had been an utter swine, a drunk with a nasty temper.

My mother and Julian even looked like each other. They both wore dark, old-fashioned clothes. They both had skin like half-dried fruit, shrivelling and wrinkling in the California heat. I could imagine them enjoying a sweet old age – he could play the piano, and she could make the herbal teas that he favored for his health, and they could putter away their remaining years in peace. And then Cissy and I...

"Ray," said Estelle, "are you going to get a chair for yourself?"

I retrieved a chair from the kitchen, feeling foolish for drifting into daydreams and wondering why I'd agreed to this overcivilized nonsense in the first place. If we'd lived a few thousand years ago, I'd have beaten Julian senseless with a club and dragged Cissy back to my cave. My mother would have lived with a gaggle of husbandless women on the fringe of the tribe, and Estelle would have been hauled off to be a warrior's bride when she was fourteen. Now she was twenty, as lovely as a thoroughbred filly, and I knew that she still half-hoped after all these years that I'd pay some attention to her. That would have been another sensible way to resolve everything. I liked Estelle, but I knew she'd never make my heart turn somersaults the way Cissy did.

"Well, folks," said Warren, "where shall we start?"

The kitchen chairs squeaked as everyone squirmed and tried not to look at each other. Cissy sat next to me but kept herself busy lighting a cigarette and balancing an ashtray on her lap. Julian coughed and breathed loudly through his nose while he stared up at a corner of the ceiling. I was working up the courage to launch into a speech that I'd been composing in my head. *Listen, everyone – Cissy and I love each other. We didn't plan this, but it's happened, and we all need to face up to the fact...*

"I have a question."

We all turned to look at my mother. Her voice sounded like a surgical saw. "Cissy," she said, "what exactly did you do to get your hooks into my son?"

If I were writing a screenplay, I'd script the following years as a montage. *Fade in to a courtroom where a judge raps a gavel. He awards Cissy a divorce from Julian. Reaction shots from both as they leave courtroom, Julian alone, Cissy holding hands with an ex-soldier – me.*

Dissolve to a map of Los Angeles and zoom in on Redondo Beach, where ex-soldier rents an apartment for himself and his mother, who has become an invalid. Quick montage of pill bottles, hospital bed, home-care nurse taking mother's temperature. Zoom out, pan across map and zoom back in again on Huntington Beach, where ex-soldier rents an apartment for Cissy and brings her flowers and gifts. Segue to dance-band music as he takes her out to supper clubs.

Dissolve to a rear-projection shot of ex-soldier driving into downtown Los Angeles, getting a salute from the attendant as he leaves his car near the Bank of Italy Building. Follow him up the elevator and into the Dabney Oil headquarters, past a phalanx of secretaries and into his walnut-paneled office. Montage of dictaphone cylinders, executive conferences, ashtrays filling up with cigarette butts. Superimpose calendar pages peeling off and blowing away. Numerals fly past for 1920 – 1921 – 1922...

I broke out of my reverie. In 1922, Warren Lloyd cut himself shaving and died of blood poisoning. Alma and Estelle carried their grief with dignity. I didn't speak to anyone for a week. I'd lost the older brother, the uncle, the father I'd always yearned for.

Zoom in on a calendar page for January 1924. Telephone rings in walnut-paneled office. Insert image of home-care nurse making a frantic phone call. Montage of ambulance and ex-soldier racing to hospital from different directions. Ex-soldier arrives in time to see his mother being wheeled in through emergency entrance. Quick cuts to sterile-masked faces, gloved hands, and medical apparatus as emergency team tries to resuscitate his mother. Dissolve to long shot of doctor walking slowly down corridor to waiting room, shaking his head from side to side. Fade to black.

Wide shot of graveside service: ex-soldier with Cissy, Estelle with Alma Lloyd, and Julian Pascal standing apart from the others. Overhear Minister's words in background: "She made many sacrifices to help others along the way in life." Mourners walk from the grave.

Dissolve into calendar on courthouse wall: February 6, 1924. Dolly back to medium shot of the wedding of Cissy and ex-soldier before a judge, with Alma Lloyd and Cissy's sister Vi as witnesses. Close-up of Cissy's hands signing the marriage license form. She writes in her age as 43.

Dissolve to a celebration that has gone on too long. Actors look weary, disheveled. Montage of empty liquor bottles. Weak radio music playing in background. Ex-soldier resting his head on the kitchen table, asleep. Cissy looking worried, smoking a cigarette. Fade to black.

Chapter Six

I found Georgie Yeats sipping tea at an ornamental iron table on the Renvyle House lawn. She wore the same purple turban, but she'd assembled a different mix of scarves and rings and bracelets. She looked like a well-bred gypsy with a trust fund.

I walked over to her table, wondering what kind of welcome I'd get. I cleared my throat and said, "Hello, Georgie."

"Raymond! I'm very glad to see you. I didn't get to thank you properly yesterday. Please sit down."

"Thanks, I will." I manoeuvred a wooden Adirondack chair into position and eased myself into it. Georgie flagged a waiter and sent him off for more tea and biscuits. She had a calm, unhurried manner that made me realize how tense I'd been around Wittgenstein. Balm for the soul.

"Now," she said, "where is your friend from yesterday?"

"He's out walking right now. Somewhere around Rosroe."

"I'm sorry that he isn't with you, but I hope you'll convey my appreciation to him. I owe you both a great deal."

"Thanks. But don't forget Tully."

"Oh, I couldn't forget him. I brought him some dog biscuits from the veterinary office." She looked relaxed and happy in the sunshine.

I said, "So how is your cat doing?"

"He's doing well. Except that..."

"Except what?"

"He's not quite the same animal. I don't know how to put my finger on it exactly, but I don't feel the same energy from him. It's as though he's grown very old."

"Is he touchy?"

"I'm not sure what you mean by that."

"Does he hiss when you try to pick him up? Or take a swipe at you?"

"No, it's just the opposite. He seems quite lethargic. The veterinarian thinks that there may be a touch of brain damage. He asked me about lead poisoning."

"Maybe you're lucky. My cat back home has turned into a cantankerous old puss. She won't let anybody get near her except me."

The waiter appeared with a silver tea-service that gleamed in the sunlight. I looked around while we went through the usual *milk-sugar-no-thank-you* business. I liked the way Georgie shifted around in her clothes. She was no spring chicken, but she was a little younger than me. She looked up at me brightly. "I hope you'll tell me more about yourself, Raymond."

"This seems to be my day for confessions. I'm a writer..."

"I knew that. I recognised you from your photo. On the book jacket."

"Which one?"

"The one where you're smoking a pipe."

"And holding a pencil? The one that looks like I'm trying to bend a black iron bar with my teeth?"

"That's the one!"

"What a way to be remembered..."

"At least you'll be remembered, Raymond. Think of all the poor souls who have been forgotten."

I thought about Norbert Davis. I hoped Wittgenstein would write a letter to him. I wondered if I'd ever see Wittgenstein again.

"...although I never forget faces," Georgie was saying. "Do you have children, Raymond?"

I shook my head. "I like the patter of little feet. Running away from me. What about you?"

"My children are grown. I seldom see them."

"You like being on your own?"

"I spent many years being gracious to Willy's friends. It could be quite trying."

At the edge of my hearing, someone said something about *Peenemünde*, and I looked around the lawn. There were six other tables, widely scattered, where men sat drinking pints and chatting in groups of two or three. Georgie was the only woman in sight. And no Wittgenstein.

I said, "It's a good thing that Ireland stayed out of the war. If they'd joined the Brits, this place would have been bombed flat."

"Oh, they wouldn't have bombed Connemara, would they?"

"No, I don't mean that literally. Why waste bombs out here? But Dublin would probably have taken a pounding. And Waterford, and Cork. Anyway, what I'm getting at is that instead of being a war-torn country, Ireland has turned into a place where Germans and Englishmen and Yanks can all sit around and drink pints together."

"That's not a new development, Raymond. They all had embassies in Dublin during the war. They didn't exactly socialise, but they did mingle a bit."

"It sounds like *Casablanca*."

"I'm afraid it wasn't that exciting. You'd see the Germans on the streets in their uniforms, but they kept to themselves. The American ambassador was furious that we didn't expel them, but President De Valera was not to be swayed. Neutral meant neutral. We had everyone's prisoner-of-war camps, and we had everyone's embassies."

I said, "I can't imagine that there wasn't some skulduggery in Dublin during the war."

"Raymond, you are a romantic. Perhaps there was. All I remember is that a few of the Germans came to our Theosophical Society meetings. And they were welcome, because our membership had dwindled to practically nothing."

"The Theosophical Society? Madame Blavatsky and all that?"

She sighed and sipped her tea. "Two or three of the Embassy people did come to our meetings. One of them said that he was a member of an Ariosophical Society in Berlin."

"The which?"

"I gathered that it was a splinter group. But Karl was charming. He invited me to have tea with him several times."

"What was that like, having tea with him? In America we thought that all Germans had turned into pillaging Huns."

She shook her head. "Karl was one of the most civilised men I've ever met. He was extremely polite and correct — a little like Willy. And I think he was very lonely. He invited me to a lecture at the Dublin Institute for Advanced Sciences."

"Really? On what?"

"On theoretical physics. But Doctor Schrödinger also spoke about Hindu mysticism. He claimed to be an atheist, but he was always using religious metaphors."

"Your friend Karl – was he a theoretical physicist?"

"I believe he said he was an aeronautical engineer. Would you like to ask him yourself? He's here."

"You're kidding! In the hotel?"

She sat up and looked around the garden. "I don't see him now, but he's here. Or at least he was yesterday."

"What's his last name?"

"Schuster. Doctor Karl Schuster. Do you know him?"

"Not at all. But I wonder if Wittgenstein does."

Georgie summoned the waiter for more tea. I wondered what Wittgenstein was doing. Walking the hills? Drawing drabbits in the dirt with a stick? No wonder his neighbors had chased him off their land. I reminded myself never to mention Auden again. To anyone.

"Georgie," I said, "there's something I'd like to ask you, but I may not know you well enough."

"Oh, ask away, Raymond. I think we're all adults here."

"If your husband had lived, how would he have felt about the war?"

She looked away, and I wondered if I'd stretched her good will too far. She said, "He wasn't a fascist, you know."

"I wasn't trying to suggest…"

"I wish that they'd never offered him that medal in Frankfurt. He only accepted it because he admired Goethe. He was nothing like the Mitfords. Or the Gonnes."

We sat there and avoided looking at each other. I wondered where I'd picked up my instinct for stepping on other people's sore toes.

"The thing to remember about Willy," she finally said, "is that he was an aristocrat. Certainly in his manner, if not in birth. It was both his strength and his weakness. And it wasn't a matter of money. It was a way of looking at the world."

"That sounds like something that Wittgenstein would say."

Georgie didn't seem to have heard me. "I know he was appalled by the First World War. The slaughter, the posturing – it was everything he despised." She flicked some crumbs off her lap. "You're a bit of an aristocrat yourself, aren't you, Raymond?"

"Are you kidding? I was born in a dump in Chicago. For vacations, my mother used to haul me down to her sister's place in Plattsmouth, Nebraska. All very hoity-toity."

"That may be true, but everything about you says *English Country Gentleman*. Which way does it work, Raymond?" Her eyes sparkled. "Are you a gentleman trying to be a ruffian, or a ruffian trying to be a gentleman?"

It had been a long time since I'd been teased. "Georgie," I said, "I'm just a hack writer with a classical education."

"For your sins."

"For somebody's." I felt giddy as a colt. "Can I buy you a drink?"

"Oh, I suppose a glass of wine wouldn't hurt."

I flagged the waiter and ordered a bottle of Chardonnay. I looked around at the men drinking pints at the tables around the lawn. I was the only one sitting with a good-looking woman. I thought I caught an admiring glance or two.

"Tell me," said Georgie, "what is it like to write film scripts for Hollywood?"

"It's like being an intellectual prostitute." I looked at her. She didn't seem to mind, so I went on. "I'll give you an example. *The Blue Dahlia*. Have you seen it?"

"I don't think so, Raymond. I don't remember the name, if I did. I remember actors more than I remember stories."

"Alan Ladd? Veronica Lake?"

"I don't think I've seen it. But go on."

"I wrote a great screenplay for that one. No private eyes. And it was based on a true story. I was in the Army with a guy named Albert. When we were mustered out in 1919, he came home and discovered that his wife had found herself a new boyfriend. She wasn't even coy about it. She had hooked up with a guy who owned a big restaurant, and she told Albert to get lost. Right in front of a bunch of people. And then she turned up dead."

Georgie shuddered. "What happened to her?"

"She'd been strangled. Albert had been a commando, and he knew how to break necks. The whole means-motive-opportunity business. They'd have sent him to the gas chamber except that one of his army buddies broke down and confessed. He'd been shell-shocked in the war, and he'd – well, he'd more or less fallen in love with Albert. And when he saw Albert's wife humiliating the hell out of him, he came back and throttled her."

"You certainly know some unpleasant people, Raymond."

"I suppose I do. But that was the story I had in mind when I wrote the screenplay for *The Blue Dahlia*. I changed everything – names, locale, you name it. I even put the hero and his friend into the Navy instead of the Army. It was a tight script, and I was proud of it."

The waiter brought the wine bottle and two glasses to our table. I showed him the tag on my room key and turned back to Georgie. "We were shooting in a hurry because Alan Ladd had been called up for duty, and we only had him for a few weeks. Then somebody leaked the plot to somebody else – nobody in Hollywood can keep his mouth shut – and the US Navy heard about it. They put pressure on the studio – no brain-damaged veterans as murderers, or there would be a Congressional investigation. Never mind that the veterans' hospitals are full of them. So Paramount leaned on the producer, and he told me I had to change the ending."

The waiter seemed to be dawdling, so I gave him a tip and he went away. "I told them I wouldn't change anything, but they came after me with all kinds of threats – a specific-performance clause about rewrites, threats to my publishers, threats to deport me."

"Deport you, Raymond? Weren't you born in America?"

"Yes, but I took out English citizenship so I could work there. Anyway, I offered them a deal. I told them I could rewrite the ending if I could drink."

"If you could *drink*?"

"Yes. Liquor. Alcohol." Georgie looked alarmed, but I went on. "I'd been on the wagon for a year. Working with Billy Wilder on *Double Indemnity* had nearly killed me, and Cissy talked me into letting it alone."

"And Cissy is...?"

"My wife. She could talk me into anything. But I felt like making them sweat a little. So I started making all the demands I could think of. I told them I wanted an unlimited supply of liquor. They didn't blink at that. I told them I wanted nurses on hand around-the-clock. They still didn't blink. I told them I wanted to work at home, and they complained about that, but then I told them I wanted two cars and drivers – one to bring the rewrites into the studio, and another for Cissy. I knew she was going to have a fit, and she'd want to get out of the house."

Georgie looked mildly reproachful, but I felt full of beans. "And do you know what happened? They agreed to every damned thing I asked for. They drove me home that afternoon. We stopped for a three-martini lunch on the way, and that's all I remember. I woke up a week later with a hangover that felt like a brain tumor. I called the producer to apologize, but he fell all over himself thanking me."

"And did you not remember...?"

"Not a blessed thing."

Georgie stared into her wine-glass. "Was this – ah – *experiment* successful?"

I downed my wine and poured myself another glass. I was enjoying this. "I went to the studio after a few days. The filming was done, Alan Ladd was back in the Army, and the rushes were in the can. I collected a healthy paycheck, and we ate lobster for a while."

"What about your writing? Did you read what you wrote?"

"No, I didn't. I decided to surprise myself. I didn't know how it ended until I went to the première."

"And did you like it?"

"Are you kidding? Now I know you haven't seen the movie. The ending stinks."

Between the wine and the sunshine, I began to feel light as a feather. Georgie's glass of Chardonnay sat untouched, creating a small rainbow on the table. I wanted to drink it in one gulp. Georgie seemed to have pulled back into herself. She said, "That's quite a story, Raymond. Why do you think they agreed to it?"

"They must have been desperate. If I'd been the producer, I wouldn't have trusted me to write a greeting card."

"Did it have nothing to do with your talent, Raymond?"

She looked at me with a gimlet-eyed stare that reminded me of my mother. "Georgie, I've thought about this for two years. They tried to shaft me, and I tried to shaft them. I wish I'd just walked out of there."

"And how did your wife feel about it?"

"She probably hated it. Can we talk about something else?"

She looked off into the distance. "I don't think that drinkers realise how much pain they create for other people."

That hurt. I felt like a kid who'd been spanked. I said, "I get sick of it."

"Sick of what?"

"Sick of being the guy who has to apologize for everything. Sick of listening to everybody else's self-serving stories."

"What on earth are you talking about?"

I sat up and looked her in the eye. "Who moved the furniture?"

"What furniture?"

"The linen chest in the old hotel. The one that blocked the door. On your honeymoon."

She gave me a withering look. "It must have been Athelstone."

"Maybe. How far would the door open?"

"Oh, not more than an inch."

"Enough for a rope?"

Georgie turned and glared at me. "And what exactly are you saying, Raymond?"

"Just thinking out loud."

"I know what I saw. And I don't appreciate your insinuations."

We sat there for a while, suspicious and resentful as two prisoners who were stuck together in a holding cell. I poured myself another glass of wine, trying to decide whether or not to apologize.

She softened first. "Raymond – if you disliked Hollywood so much, why don't you write about it? Willy did some of his best work when he was brooding about things."

"That's a luxury I can't afford. If you're going to turn your neuroses into art, you'd better be born with a silver spoon..."

"Raymond, if that's your attitude, I don't want to continue this conversation..."

"If I have an attitude, Georgie, it's the same attitude that I have toward everybody else. At some point we all have to drop the pretenses and admit..."

"Pretenses? What about your pretenses, Raymond? Why are you here?"

I thought about telling her it was none of her business. I finally said, "It's dark. I like to think in the dark."

She didn't say anything. We sat there looking at the manicured lawn for a while. Finally I said, "I hope I haven't ruined something, Georgie. When I drink, I talk too much."

She looked me over. "You're not an easy man to be with, Raymond."

"I know. Lonely men talk too much. Or else they don't talk at all."

"That is absolutely not what I mean."

She stared into the distance. I felt like two cents. I stood up and walked away before I made it any worse.

I went into the hotel bar and ordered a shot of whiskey. Before the bartender could pour it, I called him back. I wasn't ready to let The Undertow take me – not quite yet – but I wondered if somebody should stick a sign on my forehead. *Unfit for Human Consumption.* It wasn't the first time I'd felt that way.

I ordered brandy, promising myself that I'd take my time with it. The bartender produced it in a medium-size snifter. I swirled it around, wondering for the hundredth time what those initials meant. *X.O. V.S.O.P.* I'd look them up some day, when I had the presence of mind to think about it. There had been a time when I carried a notebook everywhere and wrote down everything I ran across or wondered about. Like Wittgenstein. Now I fumbled along in a blur from one day to the next. I wondered if I was just getting lazy, or if this was a preview of old age. I wanted to ask Cissy if she ever felt that way, but I couldn't, and wouldn't. Not ever. As a topic of conversation, old age was off limits.

What would Marlowe think? He and I had been apart for a while. It had been five years since I'd written *The Lady in the Lake*. I had another yarn in mind, similar to the one that Georgie had suggested – an investigation that involved Hollywood and the back-stabbing that goes on behind the silver screen, but I hadn't started on it. And the screen wasn't even silver any more. Technicolor was the new fad. No more shadows, and everybody looked like kewpie dolls.

A guy at the other end of the bar ordered a shot of schnapps. I shook myself and tried to focus. What were all these Germans doing in the arse-end of Ireland, anyway? Commiserating? Hiding from the War Crimes Commission? Or waiting for *Der Führer* to reappear?

When I'd roamed around the US before I settled in California, I'd spent a week in New Orleans. I knew I wouldn't stay there – it was like being locked in a warehouse full of overripe fruit – but I ate *muffulettas* and drank more than my share of brandies in the Napoleon House bar in the French Quarter. Somebody had built that place as a future residence for Napoleon Bonaparte. A cabal of French Army officers had thought they could snatch him from Saint Helena and bring him to the Americas. They'd plotted every kind of scheme from brute-force warfare to an elaborate hoax, disguising the Little General as a Chinese coolie and hauling him away on a supply ship. But Napoleon died before they could spring him, and the Napoleon House had been converted into a hotel with a well-stocked bar.

I took a long sip and thought about fallen leaders. I tried to remember the stories I'd heard about Hitler's bunker. The Russians had occupied that part of Berlin, but their reports were garbled. They'd said they couldn't find his body. The Germans who'd worked in the bunker claimed that he'd committed suicide. But nobody believed the Germans, and none of the Allies believed each other. Was it possible for that son of a bitch to still be alive?

And Georgie's story about her German friend started rattling around in my head. It didn't add up. His name was Schuster, and he said that he was an engineer. He told her he worked in the German embassy, and he took her to hear a talk by Schrödinger. Professional curiosity? The mating dance of the storks? Or just a friendly outing for two lonely people in the gloom of wartime Dublin? I knew that *le cœur a see raisons que la raison ne connaît point*, and I had romanced plenty of women for no reason at all. Twenty years ago I was flush with Dabney Oil money, and I was a war veteran, and war veterans didn't give a damn about anybody's blue-nosed opinions. At least that's what I used to tell myself when I went out on the prowl. But it didn't make it any easier when I came crawling home.

"I wondered how long it would take you to work up the nerve to come in here."

Cissy had been waiting in the armchair in the living room. Her eyes were bloodshot, and she looked like she'd been sitting there all night. There were coffee cups and ashtrays and food-scraps on the table beside her. I didn't say anything. I felt numb, like the way your jaw feels after you've been to the dentist, except that the numbness was inside my head.

She looked me up and down. "I guess they didn't have razors wherever you were. Or dry cleaners."

"I don't know what they had."

"Oh, come on, Ray! Don't you dare try to give me that amnesia story again."

"It's not a story. I don't know where I was."

"Do you know what day it is? Or what *year* it is?"

I said, "Nineteen-twenty-eight," and felt like an ass for opening my mouth.

She lit a cigarette and shook her head. "I suppose you just woke up while you were driving your car down the street?"

"No, I woke up at the Mayfair."

"You and who else?"

"Nobody." That was technically true, even though there'd been a dent in the other pillow and a hairpin in the bathroom sink.

"Whoever she is, she wears cheap perfume. I can smell it over here. Who is she?"

"Your guess is as good as mine."

She jumped up and threw her cigarette on the floor. "Is this the way you want it, Ray? Do you think I left Julian so I could sit here all weekend wondering if you're dead or alive? And what little bimbo has her hand in your pants?"

"For Christ's sake, Cissy, I went out to lunch on Friday with Milt and Orville and Louie..."

"Don't you think I know that? And don't you think I've been calling their houses ever since Friday to find out if they've heard from you? Maybe I should go *Out to Lunch* with them some day and get stinking drunk and disappear. And let *you* embarrass yourself by calling everybody to try to find out where the hell I am..."

"Well, maybe if you didn't look down your nose at my friends and tried to be a little less exclusive..."

"God damn you, Ray, don't you dare blame me for this! I had plenty of friends before I met you. You don't have any friends! All you've got are those lushes from work, and the only reason they put up with you is because you're Mister Big Spender..."

"At least I try..."

"Try? You don't even know how to try. You're about as friendly as a cornered rat..."

"Maybe you should have stayed with Julian, then! You could sit around in that goddamned mausoleum..."

"Oh, go to hell! And take a shower and wash that stink off yourself!" She stormed down the hall and slammed her bedroom door.

I took my time showering and shaving, waking up by inches. On the way to the office I dropped my clothes at the Chinese laundry on Magnolia Avenue. I ate a ham sandwich at the greasy-spoon next door and washed it down with two cups of coffee. I got to the Dabney Oil offices about two o'clock. Everyone absorbed themselves discreetly in their Monday-afternoon chores, and nobody looked at me. Linda wasn't at her desk. I went into my office and phoned her apartment, but nobody answered.

Cissy was right about worrying. When it was my turn to worry, I was good at it. I couldn't remember a blessed thing about the weekend. I wondered what I'd said, whose shoulder I'd cried on, or whether I'd groped anyone. Or who that might have been. They called them blackouts, but that sounded too neat and tidy. They were worse than that. They felt like missing limbs.

At the other end of the bar, two Irish men were talking about football. For the thousandth time, I wondered if I ought to try to read the sports pages. Sports were the common currency of conversation between men, and the only currency for plenty of them. But I couldn't bring myself to take an interest in batting averages or league standings. I didn't want to.

The only recent sports story that had caught my attention had been the one about Jackie Robinson, and that had been on the front page. The Brooklyn Dodgers had signed him up in 1947, and he was the first player to move from the Negro Leagues to the Majors. He'd led the National League in stolen bases and won the Rookie of the Year award. But white guys all over America were grousing in their beers, complaining about how *their* sport wouldn't be *theirs* any more. And most of the restaurants in the country still wouldn't serve Jackie Robinson a sandwich.

The men at the Renvyle bar were talking about a football match that they saw in Manchester. I looked at the map of the British Isles on the wall, wondering how much of a hike that would be. I was surprised to see how close it was – only about 160 miles from Dublin, a day-trip on a ferryboat. I couldn't quite fathom the Irish interest in the Manchester United team. They'd fought a bitter war to break away from England, but they'd go flocking back to see their football games.

It had been a long time since I'd looked at a map of England. The Sceptred Isle wasn't the natural fortress that it used to be. The English Channel might have discouraged Napoleon and the Kaiser, but the Nazis had sprayed London with buzz-bombs and missiles from Holland. I wondered how far those missiles had flown. The pub's map didn't include the European coastline, but it told its own story. *Manchester, Liverpool, Leeds, Sheffield* – the big industrial cities in the north of England were damned close to Ireland. No wonder there had been an aeronautical engineer in the German embassy in Dublin. No wonder Reuben's family had wanted to keep moving.

I put down my brandy and went to the reception desk in the lobby. Klaus pretended to be busy when he saw me coming. I said, "I want to get in touch with Karl Schuster."

"Who is he?"

"He's staying here. In the hotel."

He sniffed and looked in the registration book. "Herr Schuster checked out. Yesterday."

"Did he leave a forwarding address?"

"No."

I made myself walk slowly out onto the porch. I sat in one of the chairs, fuming. I wanted to go back inside and bully Klaus into letting me see the registration book. That's what Marlowe would have done. But Marlowe was a figment of the imagination of a middle-aged guy who was sadly out of shape, and who wasn't sure that he could bully anybody.

"You are interested in fishing, Mister Chandler?"

He was standing behind my chair. Two-thirty in the afternoon, and he looked as crisp as he had in the morning. His trousers still had that knife-edge crease. And he still knew how to turn a question into an accusation.

"Who said I was?"

"Word travels quickly in Renvyle, Mister Chandler. Particularly for a man of your reputation."

He had a glint in his eye, like a snake sizing up a lab rat. I thought about challenging him on the *Mister Chandler* business, but I felt too tired to make an issue out of it. I said, "Are you offering me a rowboat?"

He looked mildly amused, but not at my joke. "You do have a ready wit, Mister Chandler. There is someone here who would like to meet you."

"A publisher, I hope?"

"Someone with rather more influence than a publisher. Will you come this way?"

I followed him off the patio and onto a gravel walkway. He set off with a fast, competitive stride, so I dawdled a little to make him wait. When he slowed down and I caught up with him, I said, "Were you in the war, Vertsag?"

"It seems that I was too old for combat." He looked straight ahead as he walked. "Why do you ask?"

"I was in the first one. *The War to End All Wars*. Were you?"

He stopped and turned to look at me. "You're quite alone here, aren't you, Mister Chandler?"

I said, "Not entirely." My stomach knotted, and I hoped I didn't sound as hollow as I felt.

"Europe is full of ghosts, Mister Chandler. It must be unsettling for an American."

We looked at each other for a while. I said, "Who wants to meet me?"

He said, "This way," and strode off at full speed.

The path opened onto a field lined with wooden platforms on the near side and sand dunes on the other. A man with a shotgun stood on one of the platforms with his back to us. Vertsag stood a few feet behind him. The man pressed some kind of mechanism with his left foot, and a clay pigeon sailed out across the field. The man raised his shotgun and blasted it into a puff of grey powder before it had flown ten yards.

I crunched along the gravel path to stand next to Vertsag. The man with the shotgun turned around. He was thin and dapper, wearing a tailored outfit that made him look like he was on his way to a fox-hunt. He looked at Vertsag and me without registering a hint of surprise. He looked like he hadn't been surprised by anything for twenty years.

"Sir Oswald Mosley," Vertsag said, "Mister Raymond Chandler."

Mosley offered a manicured hand. His grip was surprisingly strong, and I knew that he wasn't pressing as hard as he could. I'd taken his hand reflexively, but I wondered if I should be shaking it at all.

He said, "I'm afraid I cannot offer you a seat, Mister Chandler."

"I'll stand."

"Perhaps we could have some refreshments brought out..."

"No, thanks."

We all stood there for a few seconds. Mosley said, "Herr Vertsag, if my wife returns, would you send word to her that I'm out here?"

Vertsag said, "I will see that she is notified, Sir Oswald." He turned and walked back toward the hotel.

Mosley reached into a leather pouch at his waist, pulled out a handful of shells and started loading them into the magazine of the shotgun. It was a pump-action model with an engraved barrel and a polished walnut stock. He said, "I take it that you're here alone, Mister Chandler?"

"You're the second guy who's reminded me of that in the last five minutes."

"I'm only asking to ensure that our conversation will be private," he said. "No one knows that I am here, either." He formed his words precisely, like a well-rehearsed actor. He leaned the shotgun against a low wooden box full of clay-pigeon disks, stepped off the platform and pulled a pack of Dunhills out of his coat pocket. "Cigarette?"

"No, thanks."

"You're a Dulwich man, aren't you?"

"I can see that you've done your homework."

He ignored my feint. "Were you there with Wodehouse?"

"He was there before my time."

"Pity. He would have been an amusing companion."

He tapped his cigarette on a silver lighter that looked like it had been polished within an inch of its life. I said, "What do you want?"

"No one has asked me that question in a very long time." He lit his Dunhill and snapped the lighter shut. "Most people seem to think that they know exactly what I want. And they react to me before I say a word."

"So I've asked the right question?"

"Oh, certainly."

"Then what *do* you want?"

"I want a better world, Mister Chandler. One that is inspired by the highest ideals and..."

"And what?"

He pulled a metal flask out of his hip pocket, unscrewed the cap and took a sip. He offered it to me. "To our mutual search for understanding."

I waved it away. "I'd drink to understanding," I said, "but I don't think we're searching for the same thing."

He shrugged. "Then what are you searching for, Mister Chandler?"

"Right now I'm searching for an explanation. What's going on around here?"

"Specifically?"

"Specifically what are you doing here?"

Mosley smiled. "I am searching for a house."

We stared at each other for a few more seconds. I said, "I doubt it."

"Doubt if you like, Mister Chandler, but I am seeking a place to live. My wife is out looking at properties today. We hope to find a dwelling, perhaps an older Irish estate. My wife's sisters tell us that Ireland is a lovely place to live."

"Why aren't you looking in Germany? Isn't that where your sympathies lie?"

He shook his head, miming regret. "Germany is in ruins. Ireland was wise enough to avoid the conflict."

"But Englishmen aren't exactly popular over here. What's the matter with England?"

"I'm afraid that my status in England has slipped to that of *persona non grata*. No, I rather like Ireland. There is a serenity here."

"Serenity? Is that what you're looking for?"

"What else would one look for?"

"That's what I've been wondering. Do you think you're going to find any Black Shirts over here?"

He looked me over. "Perhaps a few blue ones."

"What are you talking about?"

"I take it that your Irish history is a bit rusty?"

"So is everybody's. Unless they were born here."

"Are you aware of the Irish Brigade in the Spanish Civil War?"

"One of the International Brigades?"

"You can be charmingly naïve, Mister Chandler, like most Americans. There may have been a handful of Irish intellectuals who went to Spain to support the communists. But a brigade of seven hundred Irishmen volunteered to fight alongside General Franco. And, as you know, they won."

I knew that Franco had won, but I didn't like it. I said, "So does that mean that seven hundred Irishmen have castles in Spain?"

"No, they returned. With very few casualties."

"Is that it, then? Do you think you're going to move over here and turn those guys into Black Shirts?

"Not at all. I only want a quiet place to live."

"So what do you want from me?"

He paused, staring hard at me for the first time. "You have a substantial following, Mister Chandler. How do you use your influence?"

"Influence? You've got to be kidding. I can't influence my cook to boil the eggs long enough..."

"I mean your literary influence."

I pulled out one of my own cigarettes and lit it. I said, "People read my books to relax. Or to escape. If I can nudge them to try a little harder to get along with each other, that's about as much as I can do."

"I think you might be surprised, Mister Chandler. Surely you've read Huxley. Or Eisenstein."

"Eisenstein? *Battleship Potemkin*?"

"Yes, although Huxley's ideas are more to my point. It seems that people are most open to suggestion when they are being entertained. Or seeking a moment of diversion from the mundane."

I looked at Mosley's elegant clothes and his expensive gun. I wondered if he knew anybody who didn't live off a trust fund. "So you think that people decide who to vote for when they go to the movies?"

"If it were only that simple. No, I'm talking about their attitudes. Their beliefs. Their fears."

"I think I see what you're getting at. Storytellers tell them who the bad guys are."

"That is my point precisely."

"So what are you suggesting?"

He relaxed a little, like a salesman in the middle of a pitch that's going well. "In one of your books, there are some supporting characters from – how shall I say – the Dark Continent?"

I took a long pull on my cigarette. I'd been hammered on this subject before.

"You use an interesting vocabulary to refer to them," he went on. "*Smoke. Shine. Dinge.* Those were epithets I hadn't heard before."

"I put those words in the mouths of my characters. And they're not the characters I'd want anybody to admire."

"But you *did* put them there."

"What's your point, Mosley?"

"How exactly do you feel about our dusky brethren, Mister Chandler?"

"For Christ's sake." I threw down my cigarette and stamped on it. "I'm not going to walk into that one. How do *you* feel about them?"

"I don't want to prejudice our conversation. I'll confide my thoughts, but I'd like to hear yours first."

I looked around the shooting range. "This is a hell of a thing for us to be talking about."

"What bothers you? We're quite alone."

"That's not what's bothering me. I know who you are. I've heard about your Black Shirts, and all the trouble you stirred up in London." He looked at me with those dark, unperturbed eyes. I said, "I thought they locked you up when the war broke out."

"They did."

"And when did you get out?"

"I was released in nineteen forty-three. My wife had some influence with the Prime Minister."

He smiled. He seemed to have all the time in the world. I said, "Okay. You want to know how I feel about *our dusky brethren*? I think they're getting screwed, along with everybody else I know. Everybody who wasn't born rich. Every working stiff, every half-educated middle-class kid. And you're one of the people who's been doing the screwing. You've got the money, the connections, the lofty attitudes..."

"Now I think it's you who's overestimating my influence."

"Not a bit. You and your crowd have always run the show. Except back in 1917, when the Bolsheviks scared the shit out of you. They threw you out of Russia and a bunch of other godforsaken countries before you were able to react. But then you did react, and you've been strangling them ever since."

He looked at me for a while. "You have a succinct grasp of twentieth-century politics, Mister Chandler, if a shallow one. Let me rephrase my question. Your President Truman has integrated the armed forces. What do you think of that?"

"I don't see anything wrong with it. There was an American division called the Harlem Hellcats that fought along with the French Army back in 1917. They won a bunch of medals."

"That was different, Mister Chandler. How would you feel about sleeping in a barracks full of Africans?"

"I'm as nervous around black people as any white guy. But I know that you're playing us against each other."

He stiffened and acted offended, the way they always do. "I am not, as you say, playing anyone..."

"Oh, but you are. People like you tell the white folks that the black folks are coming to steal their silverware and screw their daughters. And you say the same thing about the brown folks, and the Jews, and everybody else who doesn't look like you. So the white folks hunker down and buy guns and baseball bats. And they vote for people like you."

"You surprise me, Chandler. You don't seem like a man of the masses."

"I never said I was. But if you're asking me to smear *our dusky brethren* in my books, forget it. My bad guys are the rich bastards."

Something shifted in Mosley – his face, his posture. It was slight, marginal – but he pulled back into a place inside himself. "I'm disappointed, Mister Chandler. I thought rather more of you."

"Don't give me that..."

"There is a price for everything, you know."

"What the hell do you mean by that?"

He looked at me with those eyes – snake's eyes, like Vertsag. "In my position, Mister Chandler, if you are not a friend, you are an enemy. To think otherwise is folly."

I looked at the arrogant son of a bitch. "I guess we're done here, then?"

"Not quite." He stepped back onto the wooden platform and made a little show of picking out three clay disks from the wooden box. He placed them into the launcher and cocked it. He picked up the shotgun, pumped the forestock, and stepped on the release mechanism of the launcher. Three clay pigeons sailed into the air. Mosley fired three shells so quickly that the blasts blended into a single roar, and three disks vanished into puffs of grey dust.

He looked at me from that cold, distant point he'd retreated into. "Enjoy your moral superiority while it lasts, Mister Chandler," he said. "However long that may be."

I took a wrong turn on the footpath and found myself at the loading dock behind the hotel. I sat on a low stone wall and lit another cigarette. Empty beer kegs sat in a row along the dock, along with bins of trash and some broken furniture. Lawnmowers and a small tractor were parked by the door of a brick outbuilding. Near a spigot at the corner of the pavement, a man was washing the hotel bus. I could hear Mosley blasting away on the skeet range. I wondered if he'd ever shot anybody, or if anyone had taken a shot at him.

My hands shook, and my stomach clenched. It wasn't the first time I'd been bullied. At Dulwich, I'd been pushed around so often that I wondered if there was some kind of sign painted on my back: *Kick Chandler. He's a weakling.* The adults had turned a blind eye to the Indian-burns on my wrists and the bruises on my legs. If I tried to fight back, it got worse. *Now you're really going to get it, you little faggot.* Basic training in the Army hadn't been much different. *If you bastards don't shape up, you're gonna end up playin' grab-ass in the Stockade...*

My cigarette tasted hot and oily, like the ones I'd smoked that night on the ship. After Billings had been called up to the bridge, I'd gone back to my cabin and downed a few shots of bourbon from the bottle in my suitcase. The rain pelted against the porthole, and the ship juddered underfoot. It felt like one of those bored, interminable nights when I was a kid, when I'd fiddle aimlessly with anything I could get my hands on. I'd once toyed with a bottle of my father's booze until I broke it, and he slapped me till my ears rang. *Do you know what that cost? Do you think I work like a dog so you can fuck around like this? Your mother has spoilt the shit out of you.*

The corridor from the cabin led to a foredeck where I'd spent the afternoons reading and smoking duty-free cigarettes. The bourbon made me feel frisky, and I began to wonder what it was like out there in the storm. When I tried to open the door to the foredeck, the squalling wind pushed it back. I put my shoulder into it and forced it open.

The driving rain soaked through my clothes in seconds. A swell smacked into the side of the ship, and a tall plume of spray shot up and drenched the deck. I felt like a drowned rat, but I wanted to see the next swell. I crouched down and scuttled over to the side. Instead of a railing, a slack chain ran from post to post around the edge of the deck, swinging in the wind. I grabbed the chain and looked down at the churning swells and deep troughs thirty feet below. It looked like a scene from a movie. *Captains Courageous*. I knew that if I let go of the chain, the wind would pitch me into those dark waters. If I didn't get chewed to shreds by the propeller, I'd still drown in my sodden clothes and rain-slick city shoes. And it would be hours before anyone would notice that I was missing.

When the wind relented for a few seconds, I crawled back to the door and clung to the handle with a death-grip till it opened. I staggered back to my cabin, grateful that no one was in the corridor. Anyone with a lick of sense, including Billings, would have locked me in my cabin. And what would they have said, or told my wife? Who would sympathize with a sixty-year-old drunk who went staggering around on an open deck during a squall? It would have been better if I'd gone over the side. Buried at sea.

I stood up and brushed the dust of the stone wall from my trousers. I was tired of feeling like a broken-winged bird. I wanted to get away from insolent rich bastards and tempting women. I wanted to go home.

I walked over to the man who was washing the bus. He shut off the water and said, "Are yez all right?"

"I want to go to Galway. Or Waterford, if you're going that far."

"I can take you to Galway, but it'll have to be tomorrow. I'm done for today."

"Tomorrow's fine. What time?"

He thought about it. "I make the run at ten. Then I'll have my dinner before I pick up them Germans and Yanks from the train."

It took me a few seconds to remember that *dinner* in Ireland was lunch and *tea* was dinner. I said, "Ten o'clock is fine. Have you got a seat for me?"

"You need to get your ticket from the desk. They can tell you."

"Okay. But did you say you're picking up Germans?"

"Aye. It's Germans I collect, mostly. They must like it up here."

"Why do you say that?"

"I never take any of 'em back."

The telephone in my room was a cumbersome black bakelite thing on a frayed cord. I picked it up and dialled O for the hotel operator. The line buzzed for a few seconds, and then a woman's voice clicked on. I gave her the number from Hubert Butler's card.

He picked up after a few rings. "Yes?" His voice sounded weary.

"I don't know if you remember me, Mister Butler, but we met last week. On the docks in Waterford?"

"Yes, I remember you. You're Ernest Thornton's nephew, aren't you?"

"That's right. I hope I didn't wake you up..."

"No, not at all. What can I do for you?"

"When we spoke, you told me about Oswald Mosley? And the Black Shirts in London?"

"Yes, I remember."

"Well, he's here."

The line was quiet. Then Butler said, "Where are you calling from?"

"I'm at Renvyle House, in Galway. He's out here looking at properties to buy."

He was silent for a moment. He said, "Why are you telling me this?"

I began to regret my hasty phone call. I said, "I'm not sure about this, but I think that he may be trying to promote a Black Shirt movement over here..."

"That's hardly necessary. Many Irish people are just as bigoted as he is."

"So are Americans. I know I'm out of my depth here. I thought that you or your friend Reuben might want to look into this..."

"I'm afraid that Reuben is dead."

A dark, ugly feeling began to churn in my guts. I said, "In Israel?"

"He never got to Israel. Or New York. His departure was delayed, and he got off the ship before it left Waterford. They found his body in the old business district."

"What happened to him?"

"He was shot in the back. A cowardly killing."

"Mister Butler, I'm truly sorry. I shouldn't have called..."

"Don't blame yourself. But I'm afraid that I feel too dispirited to contend with Mosley or anyone else right now. I appreciate that you rang, Mister – it's not Thornton, is it?"

"No," I said. "My name is Raymond Chandler."

He paused for a long time before he said, "Good-bye then, Mister Raymond Chandler."

I sat there for a while, looking at the black telephone, hearing the despair in Butler's voice. We'd looked down our noses at the Nazis. We thought they were pompous fools, a pack of clowns who'd landed at the controls of the German government through pure accidents and lucky breaks. We laughed at Hitler's ego and his Charlie Chaplin moustache, and we thought he'd be swept away in the next election. But instead of an election there was *Kristallnacht*, with the smashed windows and the looting and the beatings. We didn't realize what Hitler meant to the working stiffs of Germany. Too many people wanted to believe the myths that they'd picked up at the movies – they wanted to be like the tough guys with the quick answers, the heroes who won every fight. The Nazis made them feel smart and confident and important. All they had to do was kick a few dogs off the street. A few communists and gypsies. A few Jews.

This wasn't another *Kristallnacht*, not yet. The thugs and their backers had been beaten badly, and it would take them a while to recover. But that ponderous, ugly wheel was starting to turn again.

I hurried to the car. I wanted to warn Wittgenstein.

Chapter Seven

But I couldn't find him. His cottage smelled of stale food and clothing that needed a wash. The table looked untouched, littered with his notebooks and biscuit crumbs. The robins flapped at the window over the sink. I closed the door and walked around the dock until my adrenaline settled down.

Where the hell was he? Had I upset him so completely that he'd run away? I wondered if I could find him. Was he wandering through the fields, lost in thought? Or had he broken an ankle? Marlowe could have figured out what to do next, but I couldn't. I needed to talk to somebody.

I went back into the cottage, tore a piece of blank paper from one of his notebooks, and wrote *CONTACT ME. IMPORTANT. RAY.* I had no idea how he might manage to do that. Maybe Tommy would oblige. I walked back to the car. A sprinkle of rain made splotches in the dust on the Rolls. I drove slowly on the way back to the hotel, hoping to spot a skinny figure with a mop of curly hair and a preoccupied air, but I didn't see anybody except the sheep.

I ordered a pint in the Renvyle bar and took it out onto the porch. I moved a chair into a corner, fidgeting with indecision. The bald gardener was mowing the lawn on the other side of the parking lot. He didn't look like the man on the Waterford docks, but I couldn't shake the thought that he might be. I knew what Marlowe would say. *Bald guy, leather jacket – that narrows it down to about ten thousand Irishmen.* And I couldn't shake the thought that I ought to go back to Rosroe to wait for Wittgenstein. Whatever we'd blundered into, it involved people who wouldn't hesitate to crush him like a snail under a truck tire. I lit another cigarette and tried to think.

I could hear the polyglot chatter from the Renvyle bar. I felt lonely as a kicked dog, but I had no interest in going in there. There was a woman in California who had stayed with me for decades, and I needed the hell out of her. She'd taken me back before, but this time seemed different. I wondered how she felt about me now.

Cissy was getting sicker, and we weren't kids any more. If she didn't take her medicine, she wheezed and choked. If she took too much, she'd lose her balance and bruise herself against the chairs and end-tables. Her skin was becoming transparent, and I could see the blue veins in her scalp under her thinning hair. I wondered how old she really was, and for the thousandth time I promised myself that I'd never ask.

I wondered if everybody's marriage was a tangle. A *Gewirr?* Keeping the private promises and breaking the public ones? I didn't think that Wittgenstein would have much advice on that subject. I'd kept Marlowe at arm's length from women. What would I write about them if I tried?

The whole rickety edifice felt ready to fall. I could have been sitting pretty, retired from an easy job and cushioned with years of stock options. The goddamned booze had cut my feet out from under me, the same way that it had stolen my father's life. At least I hadn't become a cruel, woman-beating son of a bitch the way he had. But I wondered – how many choices I made on moral principles, and how many times had I knuckled under because I didn't have enough confidence? I sent Marlowe to do my fighting for me. He could live on his own, with only a book of chess problems for company. He wasn't afraid to say what he thought, and he had the muscle to back it up. He'd stay calm when somebody pointed a gun at him, and he could take a pounding.

Marlowe had come into my life after I met Cissy. Not that she was his kind of tough cookie, not by a mile. I'd never tried to write about Cissy, but I did write about Anne Riordan, Marlowe's favorite date and girl-pal. She tried to help decent people. She wasn't afraid.

You cannot be reluctant to give up your lie and still tell the truth. Wittgenstein was right, damn his abstemious soul. I knew, and I'd known all along, what I wanted to do. I wanted to phone my wife and tell her that I wanted to come back. Or ask her if she'd take me back, and hope to God she wouldn't hang up on me. She'd be out of bed by ten in the morning – six o'clock in Ireland, still a couple of hours away. I'd call her then.

I felt fifty pounds lighter. I fought a deep impulse to go back into the bar for a celebratory drink. I'd do the smart thing for once – I'd go back to the cottage, wait for Wittgenstein and hope that he'd cooled off. I'd tell him about Mosley, and about Reuben. I hoped we'd make amends. I couldn't protect him, but I could warn him.

But I knew I'd go stir-crazy in Wittgenstein's monk-cell unless I took along something to read. I found a newspaper that somebody had left on a chair. Instead of sticking it in my pocket, I made the mistake of scanning through it. The US and the Brits were airlifting food and medicine into Berlin. The Israelis were taking a pounding, but they were pushing back the Arabs on three fronts. An editor of *Time* magazine was testifying at a HUAC hearing that he'd spied for the communists, and that he'd worked with other communists who'd held jobs in the Roosevelt administration. Maybe that was a good sign – if Parnell Thomas could get his hands on some real communists to investigate, he might leave Hollywood alone.

At the bottom of the page there was another story from the US:

> *German Scientist Says American Cooking Tasteless; Dislikes Rubberized Chicken*
>
> *USA – Dr. Walther Reidel, a former German rocket scientist who is now living in the United States, has complained of inadequate support and low culinary standards in Fort Bliss, Texas.*
>
> *"It is impossible to conduct useful research without a sufficient budget and to exist under these living standards," said Dr. Reidel. "We can consume only a limited amount of rubberized chicken before experiencing the deterioration of our health."*
>
> *A spokesman for the US Army base at Fort Bliss released a statement indicating that Dr. Reidel and his colleagues are fed in the Officer's Mess, and that their diet is consistent with US military standards. He added that the Army was "...working to address any cultural differences which may exist in international research teams."*
>
> *German scientists working at Fort Bliss include Dr. Reidel, Dr. Wernher von Braun, and others who escaped from Nazi Germany in 1945.*

I found Bocklett in the restaurant, drinking coffee. He looked like one of those guys who'd never wobble, even if you poured a bottle of gin down his gullet. I said, "I want to talk to you."

He cocked an eyebrow. "About what, Chandler?"

"Not here. My room or yours?"

He got up. "I'm in 122."

He walked a little faster than me, like most Americans. His room was the same size as mine – smaller than Georgie's, and without a dressing room to retreat to. His desk was covered with stacks of documents paperclipped into small bundles. He turned them over before he pulled the chair away from the desk and offered it to me. He sat on the bed and said, "What's on your mind?"

Somewhere in the back of my head a warning light started to blink. I said, "This is too easy."

"What's too easy?"

"You're an O.S.S. guy, but when I tell you I want to talk, you say *Okay...*"

"You want me to be harder to get along with?"

I wondered if I was making a complete ass of myself. I said, "Why are there so many Germans out here on the west coast of Ireland?"

He laughed at me. "Is that what you want to talk about? The war is over, Chandler. Germans can come to Ireland. So can Americans."

"You know goddamn well there's more to it than that. If they just wanted to visit Ireland, they'd go to Dublin. Or Waterford. But they haul themselves all the way out here to Killary Harbor, where the hotel manager is a German."

"But if you were going to Germany, wouldn't you like to go to a hotel that was run by an American? Or at least someone who spoke English?"

"Possibly. But it's damned odd that they're congregating in a spot that happens to be on a north Atlantic shipping lane."

Bocklett stood up. "What exactly are you suggesting?"

"I'd like to know where they're going. And what you've got to do with it."

He looked out the window and shook his head. "You tell me, Chandler. What would you have done if you lived in Nazi Germany?"

"I'd have moved..."

"Right. *I'd have moved. I'd have joined the Resistance.* But if you were an engineer with a family and no money to speak of, would you have packed up and moved to another country? Before they closed the borders, of course?"

"Is this how you operate, Bocklett? You take the high ground, tell everybody else to be reasonable..."

"All right, let's be practical. You're working for the government, and you can see that your country is going to lose a war. You've got Americans coming in from the west and Russians coming in from the east. Are you going to hide in your basement and wait to see who pulls you out? Or are you going to make a choice..."

I didn't know what the hell to say. He kept looking out the window while he talked. "So let's say that you surrender to the Americans. And you want to keep working as an engineer. Do you want to stay in Europe? It'll take twenty years to rebuild here. Where do you want to go?"

"You're leaving something out, Bocklett. These are the guys who built the V-2's that blasted the shit out of London. They killed more civilians that we could count. They're goddamned war criminals."

"If that's true, Chandler, what about the men who built the atom bomb? You know about history being written by the winners..."

"Yeah, but we didn't use slave labor to build the bomb. More people died in that underground hellhole of a rocket factory than in the bombing." He had nothing to say to that. I couldn't resist going on. "And maybe it's going to take twenty years to rebuild Europe, but these are the guys who can do that. If we didn't snatch them to build missiles in America…"

"Then the Russians would snatch them to build missiles for the USSR. You ought to be hard-headed enough to see that."

"Christ Almighty." It was my turn to get up and walk around the room. "So we'll just keep this shit going…" He didn't say anything. I said, "For how long? Another fifty years? Then what?"

"Well," said Bocklett, "if we wear down the Russians, I imagine we'll find somebody else to fight."

I walked past the house phone in the lobby and went back to use the phone my room. The operator picked up and said, "Are you all right?"

"I'm fine, for God's sake. I want to talk to the police."

"The *Gardai?*"

"No, the police."

There was some muttered conversation on the other end of the line. Another female voice said something about Americans, and the operator said, "Just a minute, Sir." There were more clicks and some ringing, and then a man's voice came on the line. "Galway Garda Station."

"Hello. I'm out here in Renvyle House, and I want to report some smuggling."

There was a pause. "Have you observed this, Sir?"

"I'm reasonably sure that it's happening."

"And what are they bringing in?"

"It's the other way around. They're smuggling people out of here. War criminals."

"Out of the hotel?"

"No. Out of the harbor at Rosroe."

There was a longer pause. Then the voice said, "What is your name, Sir?"

I said, "I'm registered as..." before I realized what it was going to sound like. The voice on the phone said *Sir? Sir?* a couple of times before I put the receiver back on the cradle.

I gave the hotel operator my California telephone number and asked her to put through a person-to-person call to Cissy Chandler. Then I sat in the room like a guy waiting for a bus. It looked like all hotel rooms. Ten minutes after you checked out, the maid would bring in the linen cart. Ten minutes after that, nobody would know that you'd ever been there.

The operator rang back to say that there was no answer at my house. I sat there for a while. Cissy and her sister had probably gone out to lunch. It had to be that. Unless she had fallen down in the bathroom and couldn't get up.

I rang the operator again and told her to put me through to the La Jolla police. I stayed on the line while she made the connection. Even with the static on the line, I could understand the American cops better than the Irish cops. *Yes, Sir. We'll have a patrol car stop by, Sir.* As soon as he hung up, I could imagine him turning to the Dispatcher. *Tell Burgess to swing by 6005 Camino de la Costa. Guy's worried because his wife don't answer the phone. Go see if she's diddling the gardener.* She wouldn't be, but I resented a cop I didn't know for making snide remarks that I'd only imagined he'd said.

I dug Billy Wilder's number out of my wallet and rang the Renvyle House operator again. She and I were getting to be old friends. In a few minutes I heard Billy's wiseguy croak. "Ray? Is that you calling me, Ray?"

"It is, Billy. I need..."

"You want to make another movie, Ray? We did okay with the last one."

"That's not what I'm calling about..."

"I'm putting another one together, Ray. Bill Holden and Gloria Swanson, can you imagine? Fun Couple of the Year? I even got Erich von Stroheim..."

"Goddammit, Billy, I need your help!"

He actually paused for a second. "What do you want, Ray?"

"You know that organization you belong to? The one that smuggles people into Palestine?"

"It isn't Palestine any more, Ray. It's Israel. *Eretz Yisrael.* No smuggling required."

"But when you were..."

"I never said I was..."

"Okay. But *if* you were smuggling somebody into a country, how would you do it?"

Wilder was quiet for a while. Finally he said, "What the hell are you up to, Ray? Is somebody recording this?"

"Hell no, Billy. I'm over here in Ireland, and something screwy is going on. I think somebody's smuggling people..."

"Not into Israel, for God's sake?"

"No. Into America. They're smuggling Nazis into America."

He was quiet for a few seconds. "If this is a pitch, Ray, save it for Joe Sistrom."

"Billy! For Christ's sake, don't make me think I'm losing my mind! I know we didn't get along, but I always..."

I ran out of steam. Wilder said, "You always what, Ray?"

"I always respected you, you little shit."

We listened to the crackle of the phone line for a while. Finally he said, "This isn't another stunt like you pulled on *The Blue Dahlia*, is it?"

"God Almighty, no."

"What do you have for proof?"

"Just suspicions. Observations. Too many coincidences."

"Anything that would hold up in court?"

"Not a damned thing."

More silence for a while. Then he said, "Here's what I'll do, Ray. I'll make a phone call. To some people who keep an eye on that kind of thing."

"I'd appreciate that, Billy."

"But here's what I think you should do. Get your hands on some proof. Bring it back. We'll sit down and take a look."

"That might be harder than it sounds, Billy. If my guess is right, they're running a well-oiled machine over here."

"Come on, Ray. You're a screenwriter. Throw in some complications."

We both laughed. I said, "If it turns out that I really am losing my marbles..."

"Then I'll buy you a drink. At Musso and Frank's."

"And if I'm right?"

"Then I'll buy you dinner. But watch yourself, Ray. The big thieves hang the little ones, you know."

I checked with the operator when I walked through the lobby, but the La Jolla cops hadn't called back. The Renvyle House bar didn't have any bourbon, but I said that Irish whiskey would do. Any damn whiskey would do.

Wilder had put the idea in my head. Musso and Frank's – a dark cozy old bar, on Hollywood Boulevard near the Screen Writers' Guild offices. I used to stop in there for a shot or two in the late afternoons, especially after story conferences. I took a sip and thought about Wilder. He was right, the son of a bitch. I was a loner with a reputation for getting stewed at all the wrong times. Who'd take my word for anything? I probably wouldn't.

It had only been two years since my *Blue Dahlia* bender, but it felt like Cissy and I had both aged a decade. I'd always bounced back from everything – colds, blackouts, exhaustion – but now when I looked in the mirror I saw an unhappy-looking fellow with deep creases in his pasty skin. I chalked it up to turning sixty.

We'd bought a house in La Jolla, a coastal California town that Cissy had always liked. Her bedroom looked out on an interior patio garden, and she Cissy-ized it with curtains and silks and French dolls. I had a bedroom and study at the other end of the hall. In the evenings, after we listened to *The Gas Company Concert* on the radio, I'd read in a chair near her bedroom door until I was sure she was asleep. Then I'd go to my study and have a drink or two and write letters.

Before long I hated La Jolla. The women looked like lizards with orange tans and country-club legs. The men didn't have a thing to say to each other, or at least not to me. They were like the Dabney Oil executives that I'd detested back in the Twenties, without the polite distractions of shop talk. I suppose they liked each other's company. I sure as hell didn't like theirs.

And the help – God almighty. We couldn't find anybody who could cook, or mop a floor. Not to our liking, anyway. They were used to working for impenetrable rich guys who gave them orders like Army officers. I tried to talk to them like human beings, but they saw how tired and nervous I was, and they took advantage of it.

I didn't have any better luck with secretaries. I hired an old bag named Mildred to type up my dictation. She couldn't spell. I could have forgiven her for that, but she started leaving tracts for me to read. *God Loves You. Adultery in Your Heart.* I lived with her motherly disapproval for a month until she handed me a pamphlet from the Moral Re-Armament people. I told her she was fired. She squawked and protested. I threw some money at her and told her to leave, but Cissy overheard us from the kitchen. *Ray, you're not getting rid of Mildred, are you?*

Hell, yes. I don't want her around.

I've rather grown to like her...

She's my secretary, not yours. And she's leaving now.

Mildred, come and have a cup of coffee with me before you go...

I stormed out of the house and drove away. To hell with women.

The mailman must have arrived as soon as I got around the corner. Mildred brought in the letters and opened them on the kitchen table in front of Cissy. Then she left. It was a good thing that she did, because if she'd been there when I got back, I'd be doing Five to Ten for Felonious Assault.

Dear Ray, the letter read,

I haven't wanted to bother you all these years, but I need to now. I've read about how well things are going for you. The Big Sleep was great. Even my husband liked it, but I'm getting ahead of myself.

We have a son. I mean you and I do. His name is Billy, and he's fifteen. As you can see by the postmark, I moved back to Indiana. I married Dwayne. I think he knows that Billy isn't his, but it doesn't matter because he's good and steady and he treats me like a queen.

Billy is really smart, like you. But he doesn't fit in here. He doesn't like sports, and the other kids treat him like he's a freak. It breaks my heart. From what you told me about your childhood, I bet you were the same way.

What I want, and I think you would too, is for him to have a chance to get an education. Do you remember what you told me? That your education was the only thing that nobody could steal from you? Dwayne doesn't make any money to speak of, and we can't afford to send him anywhere decent.

Ray, can you put some money aside for college for Billy? We can pretend that he won a scholarship. I know you're good at making up cover stories.

I can't tell you how many times I've kicked myself for that night we got drunk together. I found out I was pregnant after they fired you at Dabney. They made me somebody else's secretary, but I quit. You go along and you have these big dreams and then all of a sudden you don't have any choices any more. I thought about asking you to help me find a doctor, maybe in Mexico, but would that have made any difference? Would I still have ended up back here in the sticks, without Billy or you or anybody?

Use my sister's address if you write to me. It's on the envelope. Please let me know about the scholarship, Ray. It would make things a lot easier.

Yours,
Linda

There was a photo with the letter – a snapshot of a dark-haired boy with a deep dimple in his chin, like mine. And at the bottom of the letter, in another woman's handwriting that I knew as well as my own: *Is this the way you want it, Ray?*

Cissy had locked herself in her room, and I could barely hear her through the door. *I'm not coming out of here until you leave. I don't care where you go. I just don't want to look at you any more.*

I checked into the Del Charro Motel that afternoon. I called my agent, and Cissy's sister, and a travel bureau. In a couple of hours I'd made arrangements that would usually take a month to organize. *We don't have any departures for England until August, Mister Chandler, but on Thursday there's a cabin available on a freighter to Ireland. Would that interest you?*

And I thought *Why the hell not?*

"Raymond?"

I looked up from my drink and saw a familiar face surrounded by a purple turban and gypsy scarves. "Hello, Georgie."

"I just want to say that I'm sorry if I upset you this afternoon."

"Don't even think about it. I was out of line back there myself."

"I imagine that other people have said the same things about Willy and me. But they said them behind my back. You're honest, Raymond, and that counts for something."

She sat on the tall stool next to me. The bartender came over, and she ordered a glass of mineral water. I said, "I'm never sure if I'm being honest, or just crude."

"Nonsense, Raymond. Like it or not, I know where I stand with you." She eyed my empty glass. "But the odour of alcohol on a man makes me nervous. When my father drank, it was always a prelude to disaster. I think that's what threw me for a wobble this afternoon."

"My father was a drinker, too. He ran off and left us when I was six. A couple years later my mother brought me over here."

"To Connemara?"

"No, to Waterford. Her family lived there."

"Are you going to visit them?"

"God, no. They're all dead."

"And if they weren't..."

"I still wouldn't go. It was like living in a funeral parlor."

She sipped her mineral water. I wondered what it tasted like. She said, "Raymond, there's something I'd like to show you, if you have the time."

"Georgie, today I have all the time in the world."

"Have you ever tried spirit writing?"

"Never." I repressed an urge to say *I haven't tried levitating, either.*

She looked me over before she went on. "When you're writing – your novels, that is – how do you see yourself?"

"I see a middle-aged guy at a typewriter. In a room with a cluttered desk."

"I understand that, and I think I understand why you're saying it that way. But when you're that man with his cluttered desk, how do you see your stories unfolding?"

"If you're going to bring up that old business about my plots..."

"No. I don't mean anything like that. What do you see when you close your eyes?"

She hadn't been Yeats's wife for nothing. I said, "Sometimes I see the scene that I'm trying to write. Sometimes I sit and wait for another line of dialogue to come along."

"And when you're waiting for that line of dialogue..."

"Okay, I think I know what you're getting at. Sometimes I think I'm in a room. It's empty, except for a desk and a typewriter. I'm sitting at the desk."

"And where is the desk?"

"It's in the middle of the floor, but it's a small room. I could reach out and touch any of the walls."

"What's on the walls?"

"Nothing. Three of them are bare. No windows, no doors. And the fourth wall is made of smoke."

Her eyes lit up. "Go on!"

"There's somebody in the smoke, or on the other side of it. I can't see him, but I know he's there. When I get stuck, I reach into the smoke. Usually I can put my hand on a piece of paper. That paper will be the idea – another scene, another line, or maybe something that I need to go back and work into a previous scene."

"And do you always put your hand on a piece of paper?"

"No, sometimes there's nothing there. But sometimes I can almost feel that the guy's handing me the paper."

I felt myself trembling. I was glad that nobody else was within earshot. Georgie was buzzing. "If you can do that, Raymond..."

"There's something else. This will probably sound crazy."

"No, please go ahead!"

"Sometimes the guy sticks his arm out from the smoke wall and hands me the paper before I reach for it."

"Yes! Of course he does! And what do you see when that happens?"

"You won't laugh, will you?"

"Absolutely not. What do you see?"

"On the paper?"

"No. His arm."

"He looks like Mickey Mouse. His arm does, anyway. That's all I can see. He has a long, black, skinny arm. And he wears a white glove, with three fingers and a thumb."

"I knew it! Thank, you, Raymond. That confirms something that I've suspected all along. Now I *know* that you and I can do spirit writing."

"Georgie, I work alone..."

"No, please! This won't have anything to do with your work. But I'm almost certain that we could summon a Guide. I've had precisely the same feeling before."

"You're not telling me that your husband saw Mickey Mouse..."

"No! Willy saw The Lady in the Lake."

Georgie lifted the vase of roses from the ornamental iron table in her room and put them on the windowsill. "Would you move the table out from the wall, Raymond?"

The evening sun streamed in through the windows. I sneaked a glance at my watch while I slid the table across the rug. It was ten-thirty. I wondered if anyone had called me back from La Jolla. If they did, the operator would have taken a message.

The cat stuck its head out from under the bed and stared at me. It was a sleek grey creature, but its eyes were clouded and dull. I picked it up, and it didn't resist. I said, "I see what you mean about your cat."

"You should have seen him before, Raymond. He was full of energy."

"He feels pretty sluggish now." I put the slack-muscled puss back on the floor.

Georgie arranged two chairs on opposite sides of the table. She went into her dressing-room and came back with a pad of paper and a blue biscuit tin. She pried off the lid and put the tin on the table. I could see thick black pencils and a deck of tarot cards wrapped in a silk scarf. "Now," she said, "I want you to sit over there. Is that comfortable?"

I eased myself into the chair that faced the window. "The sun's in my eyes."

"That's all right. I'll ask you to close them in a minute." She sat down across from me and handed me one of the pencils. "How does it feel to hold this?"

"It feels fat. When I was a kid they gave us these in school to learn to write. Actually, to print. I think that's when my penmanship went to hell."

She put the pad of paper in the center of the table. The glare of the sun at her back had turned her into a silhouette. "Now take the pencil and put your hand in the centre of the pad."

"Okay. Now what?"

"Hold the pencil more upright."

I held it straight up, with the point down on the paper. She put her hand over mine and gripped the pencil between her fingers and thumb. "Now close your eyes."

I closed them and squinted a little. The insides of my eyelids looked red in the sunlight. In a near-whisper, Georgie said *Relax*.

Her hand was warm. As we sat there I could feel the afterglow of the whiskey. I tried to ignore the part of me that was whispering *What the hell are you doing here?* I'd come this far, and she wasn't being coquettish, and I was old enough to keep from make a fool of myself. Wasn't I?

The pencil jerked in my hand. I peeked at Georgie. I couldn't see much detail in her silhouette, but it looked like her eyes were shut.

The pencil jerked and dragged across the paper again. I said, "Are you doing that?"

"I'm not doing anything, Raymond. I swear it."

I hadn't read a lot of Joyce, but one of his lines kept coming back to me. *Love between man and man is impossible because there must not be sexual intercourse. And friendship between man and woman is impossible because there must be sexual intercourse.* He was right. I felt stirrings. I was worried about my wife in California, and I still felt stirrings.

I looked at our entwined hands. Nothing moved. Georgie said, "Are your eyes open, Raymond? You'll need to keep them closed."

I closed them again, with dark thoughts. They always make the switch when you aren't looking. The pencil skidded again. I looked at the paper. We had drawn half of a circle, with two triangles sticking up on the outside of the curve. It looked like a crude sketch of a cat.

"Georgie," I said, "you're pulling my leg."

She opened her eyes, lifted her hand, and turned the paper around to look at it. "Oh, my. I wondered what that was. It didn't feel like writing."

"As much as I want to believe you…"

"I *was* thinking about Aengus," she said, "but I wasn't trying to draw him. What were you thinking of?"

"It wasn't a cat."

We stared at each other. The setting sun, low on the horizon, still streamed through the windows behind her. I wondered if the glass was tinted, or if the golden glow was a trick of the light. It would make a striking effect in a movie. Georgie said, "Have you taken a set against this, Raymond? If you have, I don't know what to do."

"I'm trying to keep an open mind. I really am. But I'll confess to being suspicious."

"Then I truly don't know how to convince you otherwise. So much of this depends on your point of view."

"You sound like Wittgenstein. Let's try it again. I'll park my Detector at the door."

"What Detector?"

"Never mind." I tore the top page off the pad, picked up the pencil, and held it point-down on the paper.

Georgie said, "This time I won't hold the pencil. I'll just touch your hand."

"Fine."

She placed her fingers on my knuckles and said, "I will ask you to close your eyes." Her touch was firm, and I didn't mind her touching me. Lots of women had hot, soapy hands. Georgie's fingers were cool. She seemed to be humming. I heard the pencil scratching on the paper, and I realized that my hand was moving. Joyce's words started rolling around in my head again. *There must be sexual intercourse. There must be sexual intercourse.*

"Raymond!" she said. "Look! What is it?"

I opened my eyes and blinked a few times. The tabletop had fallen into shadow. I dug my glasses out of my shirt pocket and put them on. We had drawn a drabbit.

I picked up the paper to get a better look at it. Something was wrong with the eye. Instead of a circle, there was a small, definite *x*. I said, "Georgie, did Ludwig show you this?"

"No, but he said something very odd."

"When? When did you talk to him?"

"A little before I found you in the bar. We chatted out on the porch."

"Good! I was afraid that he fell in a ditch. What did he say?"

"He asked me if I knew where you were, and I told him that I was looking for you, too. He said, 'If you see Raymond, tell him that I am going to bump my head in the seaweed baths.' What do you suppose he meant by that?"

"It's hard to explain. Like most things he says. But I imagine that Clodagh will keep him from bumping his head too hard."

"She's not there today, Ray."

"So who's watching the store?"

"When I was in there earlier, Walter Vertsag was behind the desk."

Chapter Eight

I ran down the corridor. Explanations could wait.

The seaweed baths were locked, but there was a fire extinguisher on a bracket across the hall. I yanked it off the bracket and threw it through the glass panel in the door. The mermaid vanished in a shower of fragments. I reached through and tried the knob, but it didn't work from that side, either. I pulled the glass shards out of the frame and climbed through.

Glass stuck to the soles of my shoes and crunched underfoot on the wooden walkways. The door to Thirteen wouldn't open. I shoved at it, but it didn't budge. A miserable sense of failure washed over me. I felt like a twelve-year-old schoolboy again, trying to swing a heavy cricket bat and trying not to look weak in front of my classmates, a bunch of confident rich guys who hadn't tried to hide their sniggers when I took a clumsy swing.

I ran back for the fire extinguisher. The chemicals inside it had mixed when it landed on its side, and it sprayed water while I dragged it down the corridor. I lifted it and banged it against the door like a battering ram. There was a cracking sound, and the door gave a little. I got a fresh grip on the slippery metal cylinder and bashed the door again. Something broke with a splintery crack, and the door swung open.

Wittgenstein was in the tub. His head lolled back over the edge like a rag doll. There was a sweet pungent smell of exhaust fumes in the air. I took a deep breath, stepped into the room, and shoved my hands under his skinny shoulders. I lifted him out of the tub, dragged him out into the hall, and laid him gingerly on the floor.

I heard the rumble of an automobile engine outside the building and the crunch of gravel under tires. Wittgenstein lay motionless on the wooden planks, buck-naked as the day he was born. I knew what to do. I'd seen a lifeguard resuscitate a girl on the beach in La Jolla. I'd wondered if he'd do the same thing for a man. Wittgenstein's jaw hung open. I took a deep breath, put my mouth on his, and blew into his lungs.

He coughed. I took another breath and blew it into his lungs again. His eyes blinked open. "Where are we, Raymond?"

I sat back, shaking. I wiped a smear of sticky spit, his or mine, from my mouth. "We're in the bathhouse. Just outside the gas chamber."

He propped himself up on one elbow. "Did we come here together? I do not remember coming here."

I took two deep breaths, went back into the room and grabbed his clothes from the pegs on the wall. I said, "Here, get dressed. What's the last thing you remember?"

"You came to see me. We were talking about..." He coughed and wiped his nose with the back of his hand. "We were talking about Norbert Davis."

"Listen to me, Ludwig. Someone is trying to kill you. I can make a pretty good guess about who it is. Get your clothes on. We need to move."

He nodded like an obedient child, sat up, and started trying to put on his pants. The hall stank of leaded gasoline and exhaust fumes.

I took a deep breath and went back into the room. The tongue of the wooden latch on the door was broken. It had been a slat of wood with a knob on the side. It was attached to the door by two brackets, and it slid into another bracket on the doorframe. Bathhouse patrons could slide it shut from the inside to give themselves some privacy. Or someone could have wrapped a length of fish-line around the knob, closed the door until it was nearly shut and then pulled on the line to slide the latch into place.

I fetched the stool from the steam-bath box for Wittgenstein to sit on. He had managed to get his pants on, and he was fumbling with the buttons on his shirt. I said, "Put on your shoes."

"I can only find one sock, Raymond."

"Forget it. Get those shoes on. We need to get out of here."

We went out the emergency door at the back of the seaweed baths. It didn't set off any burglar alarms that I could hear. The door led out onto a parking lot. There was a row of ventilator-grilles along the side of the building, one for each of the rooms. One of the grilles was missing, and I knew which room that hole would lead to.

I marched Wittgenstein through the maze of shrubbery and parking lots to the front of the building. We didn't meet anybody. I shoved him into the passenger's seat of the Rolls and fired up the engine. He coughed and hacked while I manoeuvred the car out of the parking lot and down the narrow road away from the hotel.

Wittgenstein opened the window and breathed in wheezy lungfuls of cold air. "I have a terrible headache, Raymond."

"I'm just glad that you're breathing."

"Where are we going?"

"Christ, I don't know. To Galway, I suppose. We have to get away from here."

He was quiet for a minute. Then he said, "We must get my notebooks first."

"Are you kidding? Somebody just tried to kill you. And they know where you live."

"Raymond, my life is worth nothing without those notebooks. It would be better to drive over a cliff if we do not go back to get them."

"We're not driving over any damned cliffs. But do you realize what's been happening under our noses?"

"What do you mean?"

"They're smuggling Nazis to America. From here. And I think your friend Vertsag is involved, up to his ears."

Wittgenstein blinked and shook his head. "I think I spoke to him. I cannot exactly remember..."

"When was this?"

He twisted his neck and coughed again. "I walked to the hotel. It must have been today. I wanted to know if he had been in the Austrian army."

"What did he say?"

He shook his head. "I do not know. He asked me many questions. And I think we drank a lager."

"That is exactly why we shouldn't go back. He knows who you are, and he knows you can recognise him – hell, he's already tried to gas you. He's capable of doing anything."

"Then you must stop the car, Raymond. Let me out."

"I'll do no such thing..."

"I will not leave without my notebooks."

"Are you crazy? Can't you reproduce them from memory?"

"Absolutely not. My head often knows nothing of what my hand is writing."

"Seriously? I rewrite all the time."

"That is different, Raymond. I really do think with my pen."

I pulled the car into a lay-by and stopped. "You know what you're asking, don't you?"

"Exactly."

"Do you realize that I'm responsible for you? I saved your life, so now..."

He looked at me with a gleam in his eye. "That is an interesting ethical concept, Raymond. I will look forward to thinking about it."

I said, "God help us," and I turned the Rolls toward Rosroe.

I drove the car off the gravelled turnaround and onto the grass. We bumped over god-knows-what in the muddy field until we were out of sight behind the old stone barn. Wittgenstein said, "Do you think this is necessary?"

"I think it's a good idea not to advertise that we're here. If you'll remember, somebody just tried to murder you."

"I'm not so certain of that. I may have had some kind of seizure..."

"No, you didn't. Vertsag slipped you a mickey and put you into a seaweed bath, and then he piped in carbon monoxide to finish you off."

"But where would he get carbon monoxide?"

"For God's sake, Ludwig. You studied engineering."

He squeezed his eyes shut. "I am not thinking clearly, Raymond. What are we to do now?"

"We'll get your bloody notebooks and get away from here. If someone hasn't already taken them."

We stepped out of the wet grass and onto the road. The sun had sunk below the horizon, but the northern sky still glowed with a deep blue tint. I couldn't hear footsteps or see any lights.

We hurried down the path to the cottage. The dock was quiet except for the slap of water on the pilings. Carney's boat bobbed at the side of the pier. Riding on the high tide, the boat-railings were level with the dock. I said, "I think that's how they do it. Carney takes them out on his fishing boat to rendezvous with the freighters. There are always a few cabins on board for people who don't mind roughing it. There's probably some cute arrangement on the other side to avoid customs and immigration. When you've got the US intelligence services on your side, you can get away with bloody murder."

"Do you have any evidence of this, Raymond?"

"More hunches than evidence. Come on, let's get your books."

We walked across the dock and up to the door of the cottage. I went inside, but Wittgenstein stopped at the doorway and said, *"Mein Gott."* He picked up something from the ground and held it out for me to see. It dangled like a slack shadow in the twilight. I said, "What is it?"

"Eine Rotkehlchen."

The bird had been gutted. Wittgenstein held it by one wing, and its head lolled with the irretrievable droop of death. He said, "I killed it."

"What on earth are you saying?"

"I fed it, Raymond. I made it tame. I took away the wild precious instinct that kept it alive."

He laid the bird back on the ground like an offering. I said, "You didn't kill it, Ludwig. The cat killed it. Let's get inside."

Wittgenstein started to light an oil lamp, but I told him to turn it off. He found a suitcase and banged around in the dark, filling it with his notebooks and the handful of clothing that he kept in a drawer. I stood in the doorway, listening for footsteps. I kicked myself for not going back into the hotel and phoning the police. Wittgenstein was still half-stunned, I was out of shape, and we couldn't defend ourselves if we tried. And I still couldn't prove a goddamned thing.

I said, "Lock the door if you hear anyone coming." I walked across the dock and climbed over the rail of Carney's boat. I could still feel glassy grit from the soles of my shoes on the wooden deck. I made my way along the narrow walkway that surrounded the cabin and stepped down onto the recessed afterdeck. There were wooden benches on both sides, with a tangle of life-jackets shoved underneath. I didn't see any nets or fishing equipment.

The door to the cabin was locked. Through the grimy windows I could see the wheel and some nautical charts that were half-unrolled on a shelf and held open with a tea mug. Nothing that looked incriminating, and nothing that I could get my hands on.

I groped around on the floor and found the ring on the hatch. I lifted it and looked down into the darkness. There was a steep ladder leading down into the space below. I wished I'd brought a flashlight. I turned around, found the top step with the toe of my shoe, and climbed down. It was dark as the pits of hell. I found the bottom of the ladder and the hull of the boat with my feet. The hatch was barely visible as a rectangle of dim light overhead, illuminating nothing. The air was foul with oil fumes, and the hull felt greasy with bilge. I kept one hand on the steps while I reached around in the gloom. I felt pipes and hoses that led to metal fittings and a fuel tank.

I felt as vulnerable as a bug in a bottle. In boarding-school, when I was thirteen, two of the older boys shoved me into the priest-hole under the stairs and latched the door and left me there. In the bottomless dark I'd shoved and hammered at the door. My imagination ran away with me, conjuring up putrid creatures that groped for me in the darkness until I heard myself screaming. An insomniac teacher had wandered by and let me out, shamed and shuddering in the light.

A hint of that old panic began to stir in my guts. I groped in the dark until I felt a flexible hose that was attached to a metal pipe. It felt stiff and brittle, like old rubber. I shoved my fingers under it and tried to pull it away from the pipe. Flakes of paint came off in my hand. I yanked and twisted until the hose split. Slippery liquid splashed over my fingers, and gasoline fumes filled the hold.

"Raymond!" Wittgenstein's silhouette appeared in the rectangle of the hatch. "What are you doing?"

I scrambled up the ladder. "I'm trying to slow these guys down. I want to get to a telephone and call the police."

He wrinkled his nose. "You smell of petrol, Raymond."

"I'll explain in a minute. Where's your suitcase?"

"In the cottage. I was worried about you."

I closed the hatch and we climbed over the rail onto the dock. I was shaking, and I'd never been so hungry for fresh air and moonlight. Wittgenstein hurried into the cottage, and he was coming out with his suitcase when we heard the crunch of tires on gravel.

We ran into the cottage and locked the dead-bolt on the door. We crouched by the window. Car doors opened and closed. I heard irregular footsteps and men's voices. A flashlight came bobbing down the footpath, and its beam swept back and forth across the ground.

Three men in hats and overcoats stepped onto the dock. Two of them carried suitcases. The flashlight swung up to glare on the cottage window. We ducked down, and my guts twisted. We flattened ourselves against the wall. Footsteps clipped across the concrete surface, getting louder as they got closer to the cottage. Someone held the flashlight up to the grimy window. The beam swung around the room, pausing under the table where two wadded-up pieces of paper lay on the floor.

A voice from across the dock said, *"Herr Vertsag!"*

"Ja?"

"Der Schiffer."

The light moved away from the window, and the doorknob rattled. From across the dock an Irish voice called, "Mister Vertsag? It's midnight."

The footsteps moved away from the cottage, and I started breathing again. I could see Wittgenstein crossing himself in the darkness. I looked out the window. There were four men now, and three of them climbed onto the boat. The man on the dock lifted their suitcases over the rail. He picked up a coil of hose and threw it into the boat. The Irish voice said *What's that?* and the man on the dock said *Get rid of it.*

The Irishman turned, dug a key out of his pocket, and opened the cabin door. The other two men on the boat huddled by the rail as the man on the dock handed them what looked like envelopes. The Irishman in the cabin reached down to start the engine.

There were two explosions. The first *whump* sent the hatch-door flying into the air, and a burst of light froze everyone in silhouette like a flashbulb. Then an orange-and-red fireball erupted out of the hatch, and a gasoline-fed inferno engulfed the boat and half of the dock.

The blast and the heat-wave knocked us back from the window. Wittgenstein whispered *Hölle* and crossed himself again.

The *Gardaí* drove us to Galway for questioning. They kept us there through the night and the following morning, and they used the same tricks that the L.A. police use. They separated us. They kept me waiting until I was hungry and tired and scared. They asked the same questions over and over, trying to see if I'd change my story. One guy threatened me with a long jail term for perjury unless I told the whole truth, and the next guy acted like he was my best friend. I wondered how they were treating Wittgenstein, and what kind of statement they were getting out of him.

I told the cops that I was the guy who'd phoned them earlier about smuggling war criminals. I told them that I thought someone was trying to kill Wittgenstein. I told them I was trying to get him out of Rosroe when the men came to the fishing boat at midnight. I didn't tell them that I'd tried to slow them down.

Wittgenstein's friend Con Drury got there in the afternoon, and they released us after he talked to them. He drove us back to Rosroe in his beat-up Morris Oxford. I napped in the back seat while Wittgenstein and Drury talked in the front. Wittgenstein spoke with an enthusiasm I hadn't heard from him before. *Freud's idea is that madness is like a locked room. The lock is not destroyed, only altered. The old key can no longer open it, but a differently configured key could do so.*

But, Professor – my colleagues in Dublin are expressing doubts about Freud's approach. Jung has some interesting ideas...

That is good to hear, Con. Freud's fanciful pseudo-explanations performed a disservice. Just because they are so brilliant. Now every ass has them within reach for explaining symptoms of illness.

Con Drury smiled and nodded as though he'd just received the best advice he'd ever heard. He looked twenty years younger than Wittgenstein and me. He said, *What explanations do you recommend?*

We must do away with all explanation and allow only description in its place.

Only description? Without a context?

My new therapy puts everything before us, and neither explains nor deduces anything. Since everything lies open to view, there is nothing to explain. For what is hidden, for example, is of no interest to us.

But I'm constantly dealing with patients who can't describe things because they're hidden. They've hidden them from themselves. They've buried them so deeply...

But the aspects of things that are most important to us are hidden because of their simplicity. And their familiarity.

That sent me into a reverie about Poe and his damned story about the stolen letter that nobody could find because it was sitting in a letter-rack in plain sight. Poe had pulled off an elegant bluff. He'd described a French map-game – *Find Arles – Find Colombey-les-Deux-Eglises* – where players could be tricked into overlooking the big-city place-names if they were encouraged to search for the tiny names of villages and creeks. It was a nice feint, but I didn't buy it. Poe got away with murder because he wrote the first detective stories.

And as we rolled through the Connemara hills, the voice in my head that I'd been avoiding caught up with me. I'd gotten away with murder too, or something like it. Marlowe would have spelled it out – *No, it wasn't murder. That would take intent.* I hadn't intended to kill them, not that it mattered to anybody on that boat. I didn't give a damn about Vertsag, but the others? Were they just a couple of aircraft engineers? And what about Carney? A husband, a father, somebody's son? The tires hummed and the car rocked while my guilty qualms swam around in my head.

I hadn't been in a police station since 1932, when everything fell apart. Dabney fired me, Cissy threw me out, and I took the train to Seattle. I got plastered with some old Army friends who were as lost and miserable as I was. At least that was the part I could remember. I woke up in the drunk tank without a penny in my pocket, and no idea of where I'd been for a week. I called my wife to ask for money, but her sister answered the phone. She told me that Cissy was in the hospital with pneumonia, and the doctors weren't optimistic that she'd recover.

Vi sent me bail money, and I took the Pacific Starlight Express back to Los Angeles that night. Somewhere in Oregon I stepped out onto the observation deck at the rear of the last car. With the wind howling at my back, I watched the rails rush away to converge at a vanishing point somewhere in the dark, somewhere that I couldn't see. Infinity. Part of me wanted to climb over the handrail, dive onto the track and break my goddamned neck. I'd hurt enough people, more than my share.

I pulled the flask from my hip pocket, drained the last few dregs of rye, and threw it in a high arc into the night. It clattered and smashed on the receding tracks. *Goodbye, old friend*, I thought. *I'll miss you. But I need to get along without you for a while.*

My wife was a fighter from the day she was born. She beat the pneumococcus, and we walked together out of the hospital, two shaky survivors. We rented a new apartment and began to remember the things that we liked about each other. I didn't have a job, but we had some savings – I'd never gone in for a pricey executive standard of living – and we started creating our own well-insulated world. When Cissy took her naps, I read magazines. I liked the crime stories in *Black Mask* magazine, full of punchy energy and American vernacular, and I began to wonder if I could produce any publication-worthy prose.

Driving – just driving – was our best entertainment in the 1930's when we were broke and I was trying to teach myself to write. Every week or two we'd climb into our Packard and cruise up and down the Pacific coast. Cissy would listen while I rambled on about plot ideas and names for characters. She thought it was all slightly déclassé, but she paid attention and made suggestions. Sometimes she told me stories about her days in New York, when she did nude modeling and hung out with an artsy crowd that experimented with opium. I was pretty sure that she wasn't telling me everything, but I decided not to pry. We were having too much fun.

Like the time she ran over the cop's foot. We were driving up the California coast on Highway One, north of Santa Barbara. We'd packed a picnic lunch, and we pulled off the highway onto an unpaved road that led out to the sea. Cissy had packed some avocados and a bottle of wine. Baloney sandwiches never sullied her hampers. We folded back the convertible top and sat in the sun while the breeze blew through our hair and the gulls hovered over the waves.

"Raymio," she said, "did you bring me out here to seduce me?"

Her voice was like music. I said, "I was hoping you might have some ideas along that line."

"Oh, I think I'll just sit here and see what you do." She lit a cigarette, tilted her head back, and blew the smoke straight up into the air. "Women like to be seduced, you know..."

"So do men."

She gave me one of those dark looks that made me wonder if women were a different species entirely. "What would you do if I just sat here?"

I thought about saying *I left my smoking jacket back in L.A.* or *We'd better put the top up*, but I didn't. She was challenging me a little – smiling, but still floating that unspoken question – *What kind of man are you?* It reminded me of one of my mother's interrogations. *What are you going to do about this, Raymond?* My stomach began to tense up. I said, "What would Julian have done?"

Cissy curled her lip and blew a stream of smoke toward the floorboards. "I would never have asked Julian."

I said *Oh, Christ* and looked out at the waves. I felt like a discarded paper cup.

A California Highway Patrol car rolled up beside the Packard. The patrolman took his time turning off the engine, opening the door, and fitting his hat into place before he walked around to take a long look at us. We both stiffened. He looked at the bottle and the wineglasses. Then he smiled and said, "How are you folks today?"

Cissy said, "Fine, Officer." I started breathing again.

The cop scratched his jaw. Like me, he had a dimple at the point of his chin. He said, "We get a lot of teenagers out here. Drinking. I don't know who sells it to them, but they find it."

He stared out to sea. He didn't seem to be in a hurry. I guessed he was about my age. I said, "Yeah, it wouldn't hurt them to spend some time in the Army."

That got him to look at me. "You in the War?"

"Gordon Highlanders. Canadian outfit."

He looked at us and at the empty wine bottle on the seat between us. "You both been drinking?"

Cissy flashed her million-dollar smile and said, "I only had one glass."

He looked at me. "Is that right?"

"Yeah," I said, "I slugged most of it."

"Maybe you better let the lady drive, then?"

I said, "That's a good idea," and I opened the car door. I walked around the tail end of the Packard while Cissy slid across the front seat. The cop watched her settle in behind the steering wheel. She was nice to look at, and he knew it, and she knew it, and I knew it. She turned the key and started the engine while I climbed in the passenger side.

"You do have a driver's license, don't you, ma'am?"

"Oh, absolutely, Officer. Do you want to see it?"

He grinned a lazy grin. "No, that ain't necessary. Where are y'all headed, anyway?"

He wasn't asking me. Cissy said, "We're on our way to San Francisco. My sister and her husband live up there." She put the car in reverse with lots of unnecessary wiggles and flounces, and she backed over his foot.

I felt the slight bump as the tire rolled across his shoe. He made a sound like a man who's been punched in the stomach. Cissy got flustered and shifted into first gear. The Packard lurched forward and ran over his foot again.

I leaned over and switched off the key. We all looked at each other. Cissy opened the door and leaned out of the car. "I'm sorry, Officer. Are you all right?"

The cop stepped back and looked down at his feet. "They're steel toes," he said. For a second I wondered if he meant that the steel cap had been crushed down, but he took a few halting steps. "It's all right."

"Are you sure, Officer? I didn't realize that you were standing so close..."

"No, it's all right." He looked a little shocked.

"Should we give you a lift somewhere...?"

"No!" He took more small steps in a circle.

Cissy looked at me, and I nodded toward the rear of the car. She said, "Perhaps we'd better go, then..."

"Yeah," he said. "That's right. You better go."

He stepped away this time when she started the engine. Cissy backed up, cut the wheel sharply and turned the car halfway around. I prayed that she wouldn't scrape the Highway Patrol car. She dropped the gearshift into first, and we motored back along the dirt road to the highway at a majestically slow pace.

We found a motel in the next crossroads town. Cissy steered the Packard into the parking lot, pulled the hand-brake, and looked over at me. We both burst into fits of giggles, and when I went inside to sign the register, my hand shook so badly that I couldn't read my own name.

Wittgenstein and Drury were still talking when I woke out of my doze. *Look at people's sufferings,* Wittgenstein was saying. *You have them close at hand. I think in some sense you don't look at people's faces closely enough.*

He didn't sound like a guy who'd just spent twelve hours in a police station. I said, "Ludwig?"

He spun around. "Yes, Raymond?"

"What did the cops ask you?"

"They asked me to describe what happened to the fishing boat. I explained to them that it was impossible."

"Impossible that the boat blew up?"

"No, that it is impossible to explain. That words are only pointers."

"Did they buy that?"

Wittgenstein looked at me with that dark glare. "I cannot be responsible for their understanding, Raymond."

Drury chuckled. "Do you remember the police in Wales, Professor? When you and Skinner visited me in 1939? The hotel manager saw your name on the register, and he rang the police because he thought you were a German spy."

Wittgenstein shook his head. "I have no recollection of that whatsoever."

I said, "How did you know where to find us, Doctor Drury?"

"Tommy Mullerkins rang to tell me about the explosion. He was worried when he couldn't find Professor Wittgenstein. I rang the Guards, and they told me where you were."

"Did you have to pull any strings to get us out of there?"

"Absolutely not. They were only interested in you as material witnesses. You could have left whenever you liked."

I filed that for future reference. Marlowe could stand up and walk out, and the cops couldn't do a thing about it. I said, "Thanks for coming to get us. I imagine we've created a headache for you."

"Not at all."

I settled back and lit a cigarette. Drury said, *Professor, please remind me about pointers...* and Wittgenstein said that there were objects, and there were ideas, and then there were words – but that it was impossible to describe objects with words, because words were only pointers. *But they are not pointers in the sense that a statue of a man with an extended finger is pointing, because he, or it, is not pointing at anything...*

I knew some words that were pointers, and they were pointing at me. I tried not to think about them and looked out the window as we rolled past the hills of Connemara, and the stone walls, and the sheep.

I put through a collect call to Cissy as soon as I got to the hotel. My heart jumped when she picked up the phone. The operator said, "Will you accept a call from a Mister Raymond Chandler..."

She cleared her throat and said, "I will."

I almost cried. "Hello, Cissy. Are you all right?"

The line was silent for a few seconds. She finally said, "Ray – if I was typing one of your stories, I wouldn't let you get away with lame dialogue like that."

"Christ, Cissy – I miss you."

"I miss you too, Ray. I miss *us*."

"So do I." We didn't say anything for a while. I said, "Cissy, I've been a damned fool..."

"Again."

"...yes, *again*. I thought that old age might make a difference, but..."

She coughed, and the line crackled. "Ray, what's going to happen to you when I'm gone?"

"Oh, I'm going to kick the bucket before you do..."

"That's nonsense, Ray, and you and I both know it. Seriously, what are you going to do?"

"Look. Let's not try to figure out our future over the phone..."

"Then will you come home? And stay here?"

"Yes. I will. That's just what I was hoping you'd say."

"And don't call the police any more. Honestly, when they came to the door yesterday, I thought they were here to tell me that you were dead."

"Okay. But I thought..."

"You thought what?"

"Oh, never mind what I thought. Where *were* you yesterday, anyway?"

She told me that she and her sister had gone to the movies to see Jimmy Stewart in *Rope*. She said that John Dall was brilliantly creepy, and that Hume Cronyn, of all people, had adapted the screenplay from a stage play, and that Hitchcock had shot it to look like a single take. *You ought to think about writing for Hitchcock, Raymio. His scripts are too wordy. You could really put some life into his dialogue.* I didn't care what she was saying. I was shaking with relief. She was talking to me, and we were talking to each other, and I could go home again.

I ate a fitful dinner and downed a few shots, but I couldn't sleep. I kept thinking about the explosion, and the heat of the fire, and the waves of exhilarated terror that swirled around in my guts. I wondered how long it had taken them to die. Had Wittgenstein been right about Vertsag? *I could hear them pleading with him before he shot them.* I threw off the heavy blanket and lay on my back in the clammy bed. Like an old nightmare, I couldn't get the damned Black Dahlia out of my head.

A year after *The Blue Dahlia* was released, a twenty-two-year-old actress named Elizabeth Short was murdered in Los Angeles. She'd had bit parts in a couple of movies, and she was sleeping around with anybody who might give her a break. That description, as Marlowe would say, would narrow it down to about ten thousand starlets. A few of them would become movie stars. Most of them would end up taking the bus back to Kansas or Missouri..

But Elizabeth Short ended up dead. The cops came to the house to ask me about her because she'd been an extra in *The Blue Dahlia*. They showed me pictures that I wished I'd never seen. Somebody had cut her in two, right at the waist, and he'd carved a smile into her face from ear to ear. You don't want to see those jawbones, or those back teeth. You'll never get another decent night's sleep.

I'd never noticed her at the studio, and I was damned glad that I didn't. If I'd spent any time with her, or if I'd had a blackout... But I didn't. Over the weekend when she was killed, I was at home nursing a bad cold, with Cissy taking care of me for a change.

The cops asked a few questions, showed me those stomach-churning photos, and went away. But the newspapers saw an angle that they wouldn't drop. When she was out on a tear, Elizabeth Short wore black slinky clothes and a dahlia in her hair. Somebody dubbed her The Black Dahlia, and it stuck. The reporters started calling me. *What did you think about The Black Dahlia, Mister Chandler? Did you know her? Did your screenplay encourage her to be reckless? Or did it encourage the killer?*

I stopped answering the phone, but I couldn't stop thinking about the whole business. One of the cops said that she wasn't the only one. They had a fat file of unsolved cases involving young women who'd been murdered – would-be actresses, hopeful models, girls who were making a living from their looks. I asked Cissy what she thought about men who preyed on women. In a flat voice I'd never heard before, she said, "They like to hear them plead."

"How do you know that?"

"For God's sake, Ray – why are you asking me this?"

"I'm just wondering..."

"Don't. Just don't. And if you ever write about that girl, I'll never speak to you again."

So I never did. But the whole Black Dahlia episode plucked a dark chord in me, a temptation to flirt with death. In the war I'd heard badly-wounded men begging, *in extremis.* That had ignited my morbid curiosity, and I hated myself for it. Most of us got over it, or buried it deep. But some men smelled blood, liked it, and wanted to smell it again. It got into their bones.

And if a man still felt the urge to flirt with death, what might he do? Might he devise a home-grown gas chamber? Might he test it on a cat? And if someone came asking questions about his past, wouldn't he know exactly how to make those questions stop?

I woke early the next morning and made more phone calls. Cunard had a liner leaving for New York from Waterford in two days. I packed my clothes and went down to the lobby. I found Martha Gogarty behind the reception desk, copying numbers from a pile of receipts into a book. She looked up at me with haggard eyes. "What do you want, Raymond?"

"I'm checking out, Martha. I need to settle up."

"You too? Dear God..." She turned to a woman in the back office. "Dympna, get Mister – ah – Mister Thornton's bill."

I said, "Where's Klaus?"

"He's quit. They've all quit. My manager was killed. You ought to know that."

"I do know that, Martha. I was there."

"Now I need to find new staff, and someone broke into the baths, and the Americans are checking out..."

"I'm not surprised. Has Bocklett left?"

"...and where is my car, Raymond?"

I took a deep breath. "If you'll get me a lift over to Rosroe, Martha, I'll bring your car back. I think that things will settle down now. But I need to talk to Bocklett, if he's here."

She looked at the registration book. "You're lucky. He's leaving today, but he hasn't checked out yet."

"Thanks. And Martha..."

"What?"

"I've been thinking about bringing Cissy over here to Ireland. When we get that set up, we'll plan to spend a week at Renvyle."

She looked at me with weary eyes. "No badness to you, Ray, but I really wouldn't mind if you stayed somewhere else."

Bocklett was finishing his breakfast in the restaurant. He looked up at me with those blue eyes through his wire-framed glasses. I wondered what he knew, and what he might have guessed. I said, "I want to talk with you."

"Sit down, Chandler. Coffee?"

"Thanks, I will. I'll take a breakfast, too."

"Are you asking for one or offering one?"

"I don't know if I owe you, or if you owe me. But I want to tell you something."

He took a sip of coffee. "Go ahead."

"You told me the other day that I was on a HUAC list."

"I told you that you're on a long list of possible..."

"I have a message I want you to send back up the line."

"It doesn't work that way. I only get briefings..."

"Then the next time somebody briefs you, tell them that if I have to testify, I'm going to tell the whole truth."

"What do you mean by that?"

"I mean that I'm going to testify that their whole investigation is a goddamned distraction. I'll tell them that while they're making a big fuss about sniffing out communists, you're sneaking the Nazi brain trust into the United States."

He didn't blink. "Do you have any proof of that?"

"I have friends who look into this kind of thing. I've told them everything that I know, and what I suspect. You guys haven't been very subtle. I think there's plenty of proof to be found."

He shrugged. "People have short memories, you know. If the United States puts the first man on the moon, do you think anybody will care about who built the rocket?"

"I know this much. Whether or not I deserve it, I have a reputation for sniffing out the truth. And when people find out that the government is pulling the wool over their eyes, they're not going to like it."

"That sounds like a lonesome crusade, Chandler." He picked the napkin off his lap and put it on the table. "Things don't always wrap up like they do in your books."

"You've got a point there. But stories can be straightjackets, you know. If you leave too many loose ends, you get hammered for being sloppy."

He grinned. "You just wrote my job description. *Tying up loose ends.*"

I was beginning to like Bocklett, and I wondered if I'd ever see him again. I said, "Tell me something, if you can. Why all the rigamarole? Why not just buy tickets for those guys on the *Queen Mary?*"

He took a sip of coffee. "If what you're saying is true, can you imagine the kinds of people that you'd be working with? Some of them would be church-going choirboys..."

"Damn few, I'll bet."

"...and some of them would have ugly backgrounds. But if your job would be to relocate all of them, you'd need to move some of them from a place that's more discreet. And better-supervised."

"Like a sleepy little harbor in the west of Ireland."

Bocklett stood up and said, "I'm leaving today, Chandler. But there's something that you might be interested to know. That accident over in Rosroe solved a tricky problem for a lot of people."

"Because?"

"Because even if you're right about importing talent, there would be some talent that nobody would want to import. Wouldn't you agree?"

"Like Gestapo officers?"

"Or the Commandant of a concentration camp. That doesn't mean that anyone's owed anything, but it definitely makes life easier."

I said, "Why are you telling me this?"

"I like your books, Chandler. And wasn't it you who wanted to talk to me?"

He'd won, and he knew it. "Fair enough, Bocklett. And I'm glad I'm talking to you, and not to Parnell Thomas."

He grinned again. "Do you know that's not his name?"

"No kidding? What is it?"

"It's Feeney. He's an Irishman. He changed it and became an Episcopalian. I guess he thought he'd get more votes." He reached down and stuck out his hand.

I shook it. "Thanks, Bocklett. I hope things go well for you."

"You never know. So long, Chandler." He walked out of the restaurant with a cocky stride. He was more like Marlowe than I'd ever be.

Martha Gogarty sent a bellboy to drive me to Wittgenstein's cottage. He let me out beside Con Drury's Morris in the turnaround. The Rolls still sat in the mud behind the stone barn.

I walked down the path to the cottage. There were signs and barriers on the dock near the iron pipe where the boat had been moored. I looked at the scorched concrete and wondered what they felt when the fire hit the petrol tank. We used to talk about it back in the trenches. *If you get hit by a shell, you better hope to Christ it lands right on top of you. One split second and it's over. You don't want to be twenty feet away. You don't want to turn into one of those ugly burned bastards that get stuck in a hospital.* I tried to tell myself that it could have been worse, but I wasn't convinced.

There was one thing I could do, at least. In *The Big Sleep*, Marlowe had killed a hood named Canino. He had to, or else Canino would have killed him, and a girl. But enough was enough. Marlowe would have to get by on guts and brains. Things were never going to get better until we learned to stop pointing guns at each other.

In the cottage, a young guy with cadaverous cheeks was sitting at the table with Wittgenstein and Drury. His ears stuck out, and he'd let his hair grow long to try to cover them. Wittgenstein jumped up when I walked in. "Raymond! You must meet my friend Ben Richards! From Cambridge!"

Richards didn't get up, but we shook hands. I said, "You got here fast."

"Yes. Con rang me. I came over last night." His eyes looked sad. I could see that I'd walked in on a conversation that nobody wanted to interrupt.

I said, "Ludwig, I'm leaving. I'd like to see you for a few minutes before I go."

"Certainly, Raymond."

We stepped out onto the dock. The sun was burning the mist off Killary Harbor, and the cat was prowling through the area behind the police cordon. I said, "I'm damned glad to see that you're still alive."

"Why would you think that I would not be?"

"Ludwig – thirty-six hours ago I pulled you out of a room full of carbon monoxide. Don't you remember?"

He looked puzzled. "You have asked me that before, haven't you?"

"Yes, I did. And you didn't say much. What do you remember now?"

"I think I spoke with Herr Vertsag. But when I try to remember, I find myself thinking about my dream."

"You had a dream in the tub?"

"No, Raymond. This was an old dream. I wrote about it twenty years ago. I told the police."

"What exactly did you tell them?"

"In my dream, a fearful man who was also named Vertsag was driving in a car, and he had a machine gun. He shot a cyclist – a boy. He drove on, and then came a young, poor-looking girl on a cycle. Vertsag shot her too. And those shots, when they hit her breast, made a bubbling sound like an almost-empty kettle over a flame."

"You dreamed about the hotel manager twenty years ago?"

"No, I dreamed about the man I saw on the Russian Front."

"But that *was* the name of the hotel manager."

"Exactly. That is what I wanted to ask him."

"And what did he say?"

"I don't remember." He stuck his hands into his pockets and stared out over the water. "I have always greatly feared that I would lose my mind."

"I think there's a simpler explanation. When you were in the Army, were you ever wounded?"

"No."

"Neither was I, but I got knocked out by an explosion. Afterwards I couldn't remember what happened. It bothered the hell out of me, and I talked to a doctor about it. He said that a shock can erase your memories – at least the new memories that haven't sunk in. Some details came back to me, but I still lost about fifteen minutes."

"I lost more than that, Raymond."

I thought about Georgie's cat. "It's probably different for everybody. But getting knocked out didn't do me any harm. I stopped drinking for a long time after that."

He jerked his head, like someone waking up from a deep sleep. "Perhaps I should first have to be shattered completely by a blow from outside, before new life could enter this corpse."

"You weren't exactly moribund before..."

"No, Raymond, I am seeing something. I spent many years trying to – *ausgraben?* – to penetrate to the fundamentals of mathematics and logic. I was thinking in realms of ice and steel. Now I see the emptiness of that. I would have spent my time more usefully by analysing culture. Or perhaps psychology. They seem like better paths to wisdom." He grabbed my arm, and his eyes were glowing. "I want to cut out the transcendental twaddle. The whole thing is plain as a sock on the jaw."

"Now you sound like Norbert Davis."

"I would be proud if I did, Raymond. I often quote detective stories in my lectures."

"That's music to my ears, Ludwig. But a lot of people think detective stories are 'sub-literary.' Or worse."

"Why would you take notice of their opinions?"

"I try not to. But sometimes I feel like a performing seal."

"Surely you do not mean that."

"I absolutely do. And the worst part of it is that if you write detective stories, you get pigeon-holed. If I write another novel about Marlowe, a dozen publishers will fall all over themselves to print it. But if I write a novel without him, they'll treat me like a leper."

"But, Raymond..."

"I'd like to write something – just once – that would be good enough to dedicate to my wife."

Wittgenstein shook his head. "That is what I mean about aspect-seeing, Raymond."

"What the hell is that supposed to mean?"

"It means that you do not realise what you are giving us – you and Philip Marlowe."

"I'm giving you entertainment, right?"

"Oh, no, Raymond. What you are giving us is courage."

"Courage?"

"Yes. Courage to say the things that we hold ourselves back from expressing."

"I didn't think I provided that much encouragement."

"But you do, Raymond. Especially for lonely people. You give us courage for living."

Across the harbor – the *harbour* – a farmer and his dog were rounding up sheep on a steep hillside. The farmer whistled signals, and the black-and-white dog romped up and down the field, barking and nudging the balky herd toward a gap in the stone wall. Breughel could have painted the scene. I said, "I see why you like it here."

"There is only one thing missing, Raymond."

"What's that?"

"*Street and Smith's Detective Story Magazine*. Will you send me some copies?"

"Of course I will, Ludwig. And I'll send you some copies of *Black Mask*, too.

He smiled and shook his head. "It is not necessary to complicate matters, Raymond. Stick to the good old tried-out stuff."

Wittgenstein turned and walked back toward the cottage. Drury and Richards stood by the door like two acolytes at a chapel, eager for him to return. Something had shifted in Wittgenstein, as though he'd turned a page to a new chapter. Or maybe a new aspect, whatever that meant. I'd have to look it up when I got home.

EPILOGUE

April 30, 1951
La Jolla, California

Dear Georgie:
    Wittgenstein died yesterday. From what I could gather from the LA Times, he was living at a doctor's home in Cambridge. When the doctor's wife told him that his friends were coming to see him, he said, "Tell them I've had a wonderful life." Not a bad epitaph for a guy who said that he didn't know why we're here, but that he was pretty sure it wasn't in order to enjoy ourselves.
    I didn't write to him, and he didn't write to me. I didn't want to waste his time. I thought about reminding him to write to Norbert Davis, but I didn't, and something tells me that he didn't get around to it. Bert Davis killed himself, and the poor bastard was only forty.
    I've exchanged a few letters with Hubert Butler. They caught the guy who murdered Reuben. They sent him up for life, but Hubert says that he'll be out in fifteen years if he keeps his nose clean. He'll probably spend his jail time recruiting Black Shirts. Plenty of soreheads in there.

In your letter you asked whether I ever got investigated by Congress. The answer to that is No, Not Yet. Maybe it's because I threatened to blow the whistle on the Nazi-smuggling business, which I've learned they call Operation Paperclip. Or maybe it's because I'm too small a fish to interest them, or generate any headlines.

But the best craic, as the Irish folks say, is that Parnell Thomas is in jail. That son of a bitch put his girlfriend on the payroll to pad his income. While he was defending democracy and free enterprise, he was committing salary fraud. He's doing time in the Federal pen up in Connecticut with Les Cole and Ring Lardner – two of the Hollywood Ten that he sent up there. I hope they stick his head in the toilet.

And yes, I'm writing again. It's another Marlowe story, and I'm pushing it as far as it will go. That little mouse behind the smoke screen has plenty of ideas, and if I don't reach for them fast enough, he shoves them out at me.

Cissy and I are thinking of visiting England next year. Is it possible that we might see you while we're over there? Cissy has always been an enthusiastic reader of poetry, and she can rattle off <u>The Second Coming</u> by heart. She might even be persuaded to take a whirl at spirit writing. But her health is erratic, and we're both getting to the age where we preface everything by saying, "If we feel up to it..."

Will you be in London next fall? We'd love to see you if we can.

Yours fondly,
Ray

AUTHOR'S NOTES

"*In 1947 [Wittgenstein] resigned from his professorship at Cambridge because he wanted to write and because he felt that his teaching did not have a good effect. So he went to live in Ireland, away from the 'disintegrating and putrefying English civilisation'. Much of the time he lived in a little cottage on the west coast of Ireland at the mouth of Killary Harbour. There he wrote some of his most important work...*

"*He was very fond of 'hard-boiled' American detective stories, claiming that there was more philosophy in them than in academic philosophy journals.*" – John Heaton and Judy Groves, *Introducing Wittgenstein*

The cottage is still there – built as a coast guard station, owned in the 1930's and '40's by the Drury family, and subsequently used as a youth hostel. A plaque commemorates Wittgenstein's four-month residence in 1948. In his biography of Wittgenstein, Ray Monk sketches affectionate portraits of the Mullerkins family who cared for the property, and for their odd guest. Monk has less-affectionate words for the neighbouring family who told Wittgenstein to stay off their land because they thought he was frightening their sheep.

I'd imagined that Wittgenstein's interest in American detective stories would have been piqued by the stubborn, unrewarded integrity of Philip Marlowe, the narrator-protagonist of Raymond Chandler's novels. However, Wittgenstein's letters to Norman Malcolm make it clear that his favourite reading materials were *Street and Smith's Detective Story Magazine* (in which Chandler published only one story) and the novel *Rendezvous with Fear* by Norbert Davis. Doan, the detective in that novel, is utterly ruthless and pragmatic – a chubby Mike Hammer with a Great Dane for a sidekick. If the Davis novels reflect any philosophy at all, it's a profound nihilism served up with a B-movie cast. I don't perceive that level of nihilism in Wittgenstein, although trying to understand his work feels like taking an intellectual Rorschach test.

The Doan-and-Carstairs novels may have had the same appeal for Wittgenstein as the Betty Hutton musicals and the Tom Mix westerns that he loved. He'd sit in the centre of the front row in the cinema, letting the movies wash over him like a shower. The Davis novels, which have been re-issued as e-books by Book Revivals Press, share that uncritical holiday-from-worry quality.

Did Wittgenstein read Raymond Chandler? Chandler's prose has a roller-coaster quality like the movies that Wittgenstein enjoyed, sweeping his readers past improbabilities and coincidences and unseemly twentieth-century-white-male prejudices. Chandler acknowledged the addictive quality of his prose – he said that the talent to produce it was something that a writer was born with, "like red hair" – and he enjoyed reading his own work. In *Pool of Darkness* I claim that Wittgenstein was familiar with Chandler's novels, but I wonder if in fact he was. As Ray Monk describes it, "...when Malcolm sent him some other brand [of magazine, not *Street & Smith's*], Wittgenstein gently admonished him, asking why he had tried to be original instead of sticking to the 'good old tried out stuff.'" – Ray Monk, *Ludwig Wittgenstein: The Duty of Genius*

"...I often found myself thinking of them, of their oddly affecting relationship, and their strangely peripatetic lives, Cissy's mysterious allure, Chandler's inconsolable grief at her death, and the strangely enduring bond that had held them together for so many years... I was not looking to create a fictional relationship, and yet I wanted to be free to imagine their lives. I wanted to know them so intimately that it would amount to a kind of haunting." – Judith Freeman, *The Long Embrace: Raymond Chandler and the Woman He Loved*

Raymond Chandler probably spent the summer of 1948 at his home in La Jolla, California, licking his Hollywood wounds and writing *The Little Sister*. He had tested his wife's patience by having another fling with a secretary, a favourite target of shy men. Cissy's health was deteriorating, and between their quirks and crotchets they weren't able to retain household staff. During the day Chandler wrote and cooked and did the housekeeping, and in the evening he and his wife listened to the *Gas Company Evening Concert* on the radio. After Cissy went to bed, he wrote hundreds of letters. Frank McShane, who wrote the 1976 biography of Raymond Chandler, also selected and edited a collection of Chandler's letters in 1987. There's a gap in that collection between June 9th and July 28th. It's not impossible that Chandler ran off to Ireland for a few weeks between those dates, but I wouldn't attempt to defend that notion in a dissertation review.

The Long Embrace: Raymond Chandler and the Woman He Loved, Judith Freeman's personal investigation of Chandler's life and relationships, should stand alongside the Marlowe novels on the bookshelf of every Chandler fan. I am also deeply indebted to Josef Hoffman for his article on *Hard-Boiled Wit:*

Ludwig Wittgenstein and Norbert Davis. For a sobering biographical sketch, see *Norbert Davis: Profile of a Pulp Writer* by John L. Apostolou. I also appreciate the generosity of Professor Alan Titley of University College Cork in letting me read a copy of *LUDO*, his unpublished play about Wittgenstein's self-imposed exiles in Norway and in Ireland, and for recommending Tim Robinson's *Connemara: The Last Pool of Darkness*, another exceptional blend of history, geography, personal experience and a great deal more.

Oscar Carl Holderer died Tuesday in Huntsville, Alabama… Born in Germany the year after World War I ended, Holderer came to the United States in 1945 with a group of 120 rocket engineers led by Wernher von Braun. Their move was part of a project called Operation Paperclip that transferred technology for the German V-2 and other rockets to the United States. – The Los Angeles Times, May 6, 2015

There is no evidence to suggest that former Nazis were smuggled to North America specifically through Killary Harbour in County Galway, Ireland. Operation Paperclip, however, a programme originated by the US Joint Intelligence Objectives Agency, continued from the end of World War Two until 1990, "bleaching" the records of former Nazis. Over 1,600 German scientists and military officers, along with their families, were granted security clearances and brought quietly from various European locations into the United States.

In 1958, the year before he died, Raymond Chandler lived in a London hotel next door to the Irish writer Bill Long. In "Old Yellow Gloves," the first chapter of *Brief Encounters: Meetings with Remarkable People*, Long recalls conversations with Chandler about the Irish city of Waterford, where they had both spent their boyhoods and school vacations. They both had fond memories of a bookshop in the maze of streets near the docks, where the younger Long had bought his copies of Chandler's *Farewell, My Lovely* and *The High Window*. Owned by a family named Powers, the bookstore had been known to its dedicated customers as "Stickyback's" for reasons that neither Chandler nor Long could recall.

According to Bill Long, Raymond Chandler speculated about writing a Philip Marlowe story that would be set in Ireland. "He explained that he had been thinking about that old bookshop, about the maze of narrow streets in which it was located, and had thought about how wonderful it would be to use it as a setting for a new Philip Marlowe book. And before I could react or comment, he was off into the detail ... *Marlowe on vacation in Ireland ... stops over for a few days in Waterford ... finds an old pub he likes on the quays ... drinking there, witnesses a brawl between sailors from different ships ... next day hears one of them has been murdered ... his body dumped in the doorway of the book shop ... that night, drinking in the same pub, Marlowe, recognised by the American skipper of the victim's ship, agrees to do a little investigative work ...*"

The elegiac tone of Long's memoir confirms Judith Freeman's chapter on Chandler's lonely peregrinations between California and England after his wife died. But he still showed flashes of the brash forty-four-year-old ex-oil executive who decided to try his hand at crafting the American vernacular into hard-boiled stories for *Black Mask* magazine:

"*Any man,*" [Chandler] said wearily, but with great conviction, "*who can write a page of living prose adds something to our life, illuminates the dark a bit for others. And I could do that, I could do that... once. You know, Bill, an artist can never deny his art. Indeed, he would never want to. Why should he? For, you see, if you believe in an ideal, you don't own it. It owns you!*"

– Tom Sigafoos
County Leitrim, Ireland
January 2024

SOURCES

- Apostolou, John L. – *Norbert Davis: Profile of a Pulp Writer*, originally published in *The Armchair Detective VOL 15 #1 1982* and reprinted with revisions and corrections in BlackMaskMagazine.com (http://www.blackmaskmagazine.com/bm_03.html)
- Beckman, Morris – *The 43 Group: Battling with Mosley's Blackshirts*. The History Press, 2013. EPUB ISBN 978-0-7524-9979-6.
- Chandler, Raymond – *Selected Letters of Raymond Chandler*, edited by Frank McShane. Delta Books / Dell Publishing, 1987. ISBN 0-385-29531-6
- Chandler, Raymond – *The High Window*, in *The Raymond Chandler Omnibus*. Random House, 1964. ISBN 978-0394413198
- Davis, Norbert – *The Doan and Carstairs Novels*. Book Revivals Press, 2013. ASIN: B00C6LJCMS
- Drury, Maurice O'Connor – *The Danger of Words*. Routledge & Kegan Paul Ltd, 1973. ISBN 0-7100-7596-0
- Freeman, Judith – *The Long Embrace: Raymond Chandler and the Woman He Loved*. Vintage Books, 2008. ISBN 978-1-4000-9517-9
- Goodrick-Clarke, Nicholas – *The Occult Roots of Nazism*. I.B. Tauris & Co Ltd, 2004. ISBN 1 86064 973 4
- Heaton, John and Groves, Judy – *Introducing Wittgenstein*. Icon Books Ltd., 2005. ISBN 1 84046 641 33

- Hiney, Tom – *Raymond Chandler: A Biography.* Vintage Books, 1998. ISBN: 978-0099533511
- Hoffman, Josef – *Hard-Boiled Wit: Ludwig Wittgenstein and Norbert Davis,* in CADS (Crime and Detective Stories) Magazine #44, October 2003 (http://www.mysteryfile.com/NDavis/Wit.html)
- Long, Bill – *Brief Encounters: Meetings with Remarkable People.* New Island Books, 1999. ISBN 1 874597 84 7
- Monk, Ray – *Ludwig Wittgenstein: The Duty of Genius.* Vintage Books, 1991. ISBN 9780099883708
- Robinson, Tim – *Connemara: The Last Pool of Darkness.* Penguin Ireland, 2008. ISBN 978-1844881550
- Saddlemyer, Ann – *Becoming George: The Life of Mrs W.B. Yeats.* Oxford University Press, 2002. ISBN 0-19-926921-1
- Titley, Alan – *LUDO,* an unpublished play in two acts. Dr Titley is Emeritus Professor of Modern Irish, University College Cork.
- Walsh, Maurice – *Mosley in Ireland,* in *The Dublin Review,* issue No. 26, Spring 2007
- Williams, Tom – *Raymond Chandler: A Mysterious Something in the Light: A Life.* Chicago Review Press, 2013. ISBN 978-1613748404
- Wittgenstein, Ludwig – *Culture and Value, Revised Edition,* edited by G.H. von Wright. Blackwell Publishers, 1998. ISBN 0-631-20571-3

ACKNOWLEDGEMENTS

I would like to express my appreciation to:

- Declan Burke, novelist and crime fiction reviewer for The Irish Times.

- Alan Titley, Emeritus Professor of Modern Irish, University College Cork. Dr Titley is the author of *Lámh, Lámh Eile,* a noir-flavoured private-eye novel in the Irish language, and many other translations and creative works.

- Fintan Power, author and writing mentor, who hosted a fascinating walking tour of the Chandler-related sites of Waterford.

- Judith Freeman, author of *The Long Embrace: Raymond Chandler and the Woman He Loved,* for her suggestions and encouragement.

And to Monica Corish, without whom none of this would amount to a hill of beans in this crazy world.

About the Author

Creative nonfiction and short stories by Irish-American author Tom Sigafoos have appeared in *The Quiet Quarter Anthology: Ten Years of Great Irish Writing, Crannog Literary Magazine, The Cathach Literary Journal, The Leitim Guardian, The Irish Times, *82 Review, Authors Publish Magazine, Trasna, The Ekphrastic Review, Loughshore Lines, Sunshine Superhighway: Solar Sailings* and *History Ireland*.

An early version of *Pool of Darkness* was shortlisted for the Penny Dreadful Novella Prize.

Tom Sigafoos is the author of *The Cursing Stone*, an Irish historical novel based on the shipwreck of the British gunboat *HMS Wasp* during the Irish Land Wars. The opening chapter of *The Cursing Stone* was published in *The Copperfield Review* under the title *Egging*.

His first crime novel, *Code Blue*, is available on Amazon. His radio memoir *An American Scrapbook* is posted on SoundCloud.

A member of WORD, the Irish Writers' Centre and the Irish Writers' Union, he has served as Chair and PRO of the Allingham Arts Association.

Pool of Darkness – Raymond Chandler in Ireland is also available as a Kindle e-book and as an audiobook.

For additional information see www.tomsigafoos.com

Author portrait by John Ford, Cincinnati OH